SPECIAL MESSAGE TO READERS

This book is published under the auspices of

THE ULVERSCROFT FOUNDATION

(registered charity No. 264873 UK)

Established in 1972 to provide funds for research, diagnosis and treatment of eye diseases.

Examples of contributions made are: —

A Children's Assessment Unit at Moorfield's Hospital, London.

•

Twin operating theatres at the Western Ophthalmic Hospital, London.

•

A Chair of Ophthalmology at the Royal Australian College of Ophthalmologists.

•

The Ulverscroft Children's Eye Unit at the Great Ormond Street Hospital For Sick Children, London.

You can help further the work of the Foundation by making a donation or leaving a legacy. Every contribution, no matter how small, is received with gratitude. Please write for details to:

THE ULVERSCROFT FOUNDATION,
The Green, Bradgate Road, Anstey,
Leicester LE7 7FU, England.
Telephone: (0116) 236 4325

In Australia write to:

THE ULVERSCROFT FOUNDATION,
c/o The Royal Australian College of Ophthalmologists,
27, Commonwealth Street, Sydney,
N.S.W. 2010.

THE OUTLAWED DEPUTY

Cassidy Yates was appointed deputy sheriff of Redemption City, but such was his knack of attracting trouble that barely twenty-four hours after his appointment he had been slapped into jail! And if that wasn't bad enough, Brett McBain's outlaw gang ride into town to bust Nathaniel McBain from jail. Sheriff Wishbone is killed and the townsfolk think Cassidy is responsible. The only way for Cassidy to prove his innocence is to infiltrate Brett's gang . . .

I. J. PARNHAM

THE OUTLAWED DEPUTY

Complete and Unabridged

LINFORD
Leicester

First published in Great Britain in 2001 by
Robert Hale Limited
London

First Linford Edition
published 2003
by arrangement with
Robert Hale Limited
London

British Library CIP Data

Parnham, I. J.
The outlawed deputy.—Large print ed.—
Linford western library
1. Western stories
2. Large type books
I. Title
823.9′2 [F]

ISBN 0–7089–9438–5

Published by
F. A. Thorpe (Publishing)
Anstey, Leicestershire

Set by Words & Graphics Ltd.
Anstey, Leicestershire
Printed and bound in Great Britain by
T. J. International Ltd., Padstow, Cornwall

This book is printed on acid-free paper

1

Through narrowed eyes, Cassidy stared at the three playing cards clutched in his right hand. He held an ace and two jacks, and with two aces included in the five hold cards on the table, he knew that his poker hand was strong. After playing for two hours he could read the worried expressions of his three opponents, and knew that from the final deal, they didn't have anything to beat his hand. With everything being equal, he should risk betting whatever it took to win the pot.

Unfortunately, Cassidy knew everything wasn't equal. The sallow-faced Jake Grounding, sitting on his left, was clearly colluding with the gaunt, balding George Rogers, sitting on his right, and Bill McGruder, sitting opposite, cheated all on his own. Cassidy watched Bill finger his cards, slowly moving each front card to the back, as he had each time that he'd swapped a card from his identical, secreted pack in the inside pocket of his short, heavily brocaded jacket.

Bill McGruder smirked, leant back in his chair, patted his ample stomach and, while staring at Cassidy over the top of his cards, muttered:

'We're all waiting for you, Cassidy. What you going to do?'

While pondering his next action, Cassidy adjusted his red bandanna, shuffled further into his buckskin jacket, and glanced around the room. He sat at a small, battered circular table by the wall, where his group of fellow card-players represented the only customers in Roger's Saloon tonight. This saloon was a dusty, starkly furnished, drinking establishment in the middle of Redemption City. Here, even late in the summer and with the sun still up, the room had an airy chill that only a permanent lack of patrons could bring.

Starved of entertainment, in a town

singularly lacking in anything to interest a man who'd been on the trail from Beaver Ridge for six straight days, Cassidy had readily accepted Bill McGruder's offer to play poker. Despite the cheating, Cassidy had decided to stay, as having Bill try to steal his money was more entertaining than sitting on his own.

For the last time Cassidy glanced at his cards. Faced with such an obvious group of cheating opponents, he ought to fold. He was up ten dollars on the evening, but with a twenty-dollar pot, the highest so far, Cassidy felt temptation batter at him. Having made his decision, Cassidy favoured Bill with his most confident smile.

'I'm in too, show us what you've got,' he said.

After counting out, and throwing three dollars on to the table, Cassidy glared at Bill, waiting to see how far he'd dared to cheat. While fingering his neatly trimmed moustache, Bill licked his fat lips and with a flourish laid his cards down to a chorus of whistles from Jake and George as they stared at his six, seven and jack of hearts. Bill's cards, when combined with the nine and two of hearts in the hold cards, provided a good flush.

'Beats me,' George said, throwing his cards down.

'Yup, me too,' Jake said, throwing his cards on top of George's.

Wincing, Cassidy stared at his own cards, which included another, authentically dealt, jack of hearts. He'd previously considered Bill a practised cheat, but clearly, Cassidy had overestimated his abilities.

Thoughtfully, Cassidy stared at Jake and George, trying to judge if they were in league with Bill. Cassidy watched Jake lean over the table, staring at Bill's cards, as if by staring hard enough, he could suddenly make the heart flush become a worse hand, and George stared into space lost in his own thoughts. Unfortunately, Cassidy couldn't tell if their postures meant they knew what Bill had just done. In his thirty years, Cassidy had played many hands of poker, in many different towns, and encountered all manner of underhand dealing. Each occasion was different. He had to judge each situation on its merits, and this time he decided on caution; the pot wasn't high enough to complain about and he'd enjoyed his early evening's entertainment.

Smiling, Cassidy said, 'Beats me too, I'll call it a night.'

With a resigned wave of his hand, Cassidy threw his cards on top of the others, face down, and pushed from the table. Standing, he tinkled his profits into his pocket. Having come into Roger's Saloon down to his last five dollars, he could walk out with twelve. Cassidy judged this a good profit. He touched his fingers to his low-crowned Stetson, and swirled away. He felt ready now to seek a different saloon for the rest of his night's drinking in Redemption City, if such a dead-end place as this included another saloon.

When Cassidy had strolled half-way to the door, from behind him, he heard Bill shout:

'What's this? You've been holding out on us.'

Instantly, Cassidy swivelled round to see Bill had turned over Cassidy's cards. Bill brandished both jacks of hearts, then slammed them down on the table, and glared at him, his jowls wobbling as he threw open his mouth in mock astonishment. Cassidy sighed, as Bill went even further down in his estimation. Successfully cheating was one matter, but this was stupidity.

Annoyed, Cassidy sauntered back, and leaning over the table, his face inches from Bill's, muttered, 'I'm surprised you want to let everyone know just what you've been up to.'

Leaning back in his chair, Bill glanced around the table at Jake and George, smirking at each in turn.

'What I've been doing is putting up with your cheating all evening. I reckon that as soon as you saw I'd the real jack of hearts in my hand, you couldn't let us know what you'd done, so you threw in your cards. Lucky I'd spotted you cheating earlier.'

After allowing his head to drop, Cassidy pushed himself from the table, and slowly turned to George.

'Bill here has a duplicate pack of cards in the inside pocket of his jacket.'

'You calling me a cheat?' Bill muttered.

'Nope,' Cassidy said, slowly turning his gaze back to Bill. 'I'm calling you a bad cheat.'

With his yellowing teeth bared, Bill whispered, 'Prove it.'

Carefully watching his every movement, Cassidy stared at Bill as he lifted his podgy hands, pressed his palms to his chest, and ran them gently down his jacket, smoothing the material flat to his rounded stomach. Not waiting for Bill to finish his actions, Cassidy nodded to himself, his suspicions were right, Bill was in league with Jake and

George, and the duplicate pack had already changed hands.

Shaking his head, Cassidy muttered, 'You took a lot of trouble to try and trick me out of my last few dollars. You ought to choose the people you cheat with more care, if you want to make real money.'

George glared at him, and said, 'Forget the talk, I believe Bill, and you're not walking out of here with my money.'

Dismayed by the turn of events, Cassidy muttered, 'That's the way you treat strangers around these parts, is it?'

'Only the type we don't like, and we don't take kindly to cheats,' George said, staring deep into Cassidy's eyes.

With a sigh, Cassidy slowly slipped his hand into his pocket, pulled out his twelve dollars, and slammed the coins on to the table.

'Will this compensate you?'

George smirked, and dashed a surprised looking glance at Jake and Bill,

'Sure will.'

The second George's scrawny hand pounced on the coins, Cassidy hit him with the back of his right hand across the cheek, the slap echoing around the empty saloon. With his left hand, he grabbed the table, launching it to his left to catch Jake full in the chest. As Bill staggered to his feet to avoid the spinning table, Cassidy grabbed his Colt Peacemaker from his holster, and with a swirl of his hand, set the barrel firmly on Bill.

With a practised gaze, Cassidy glanced at George and Jake rolling on the floor, making sure they didn't try anything more. Having seized control of the situation, Cassidy stared at Bill, and smiled.

'Now that things are a little clearer, what were you saying about cheating?'

With his feet set wide, Bill hissed, 'I said, you're a cheat.'

Cassidy gulped. He had no desire to kill, not in this situation. 'A twenty-dollar pot ain't worth dying for, Bill.

Give me the last pot, and this goes no further.'

Squaring his stance, Bill muttered, 'Maybe there's only a twenty-dollar pot at stake, but this is worth dying for, when I won't be doing the dying.'

Simultaneously, he saw Bill's gaze flicker over his left shoulder, and from behind him, Cassidy heard a tell-tale click. Knowing exactly the location of the cocked gun, Cassidy spun round, falling to one knee as he turned to confuse his assailant, and found he stared directly at a gun, and behind the gun, a man with a star.

The man with the star glared at Cassidy.

'The name's Wishbone, Sheriff of Redemption City. Put your gun down, stranger, real slow, or die.'

After a quick glance over his shoulder, to make sure the other card players weren't about to attack him, Cassidy nodded. Although the sheriff was shorter than the medium-built Cassidy, and at least ten years older, with tufts of streaked grey hair poking from under his dark Stetson, the assurance in Wishbone's gaze convinced Cassidy that no one would cross him and live.

For a moment Cassidy stared at the sheriff's .45, and, keeping his movements deliberately slow, spun his Peacemaker on his finger. With the barrel pointed at his own chest, he placed his gun on the floor, then kicked it to Sheriff Wishbone. Still keeping his movements slow, Cassidy lifted both hands until they touched the brim of his Stetson. He knew the routine.

Sheriff Wishbone dropped to one knee and grabbed Cassidy's Peacemaker, all the time keeping his .45 trained on Cassidy. Then, stepping aside, he waved at Cassidy to follow him.

'He cheated us, tried to take everything we had,' Bill whined as Cassidy shuffled towards the saloon doors.

'Of course, Bill, of course he did,' Sheriff Wishbone said, nodding at Bill. 'Lucky I came along when I did, before he took more than just your money.'

As he strode by Sheriff Wishbone, with his hands on his head, Cassidy said, 'I'm no cheat. I'm innocent.'

Sheriff Wishbone snorted, and pushed him forward a few paces with the toe of his boot. 'Course you are, and after a couple of nights in the cells to cool off, we'll no longer need to worry who was in the right.'

In surprise that they were leaving without Bill and the others, Cassidy asked, 'Ain't you going to arrest Bill?'

'Don't see him pointing no gun, because he knows my rules. Nobody threatens another man with more than their fists in my town.'

As he shuffled across the road to the sheriff's office diagonally opposite the saloon, Cassidy allowed his head to drop in resignation, and muttered, 'Fair enough, I suppose.'

With this submission, Sheriff Wishbone asked, 'What's your name, stranger?'

Standing outside the sheriff's office, Cassidy slowly took his hands from his Stetson, set them on his hips, and smiled at Sheriff Wishbone.

'I'm Cassidy Yates.'

Sheriff Wishbone narrowed his eyes.

'Cassidy? Where have I heard that name before?'

Cassidy laughed, his voice sounding a little hollow.

'Probably because Marshal Devine told you I was coming here.'

'Why would you know Marshal Devine?'

Smiling, while he appraised Sheriff Wishbone, Cassidy muttered: 'Because he sent me here to be your new deputy.'

* * *

At his office, Sheriff Wishbone pushed his new deputy through the door.

'Hey, there's no need for that,'

Cassidy whined.

Sheriff Wishbone's new deputy was a few days early reporting for duty and, while closing the door, the sheriff decided that he could put his early arrival to good use.

'Sure is. Like I said, a couple of nights in the cells should help to cool you down.'

If there was one thing Sheriff Wishbone couldn't stand, it was a lawman trying to take advantage of his position to flout the law. With luck, Cassidy would learn that lesson before he'd even sworn him in.

'But that Bill McGruder cheated me; you can't expect anyone to ignore that, deputy or no deputy.'

Sheriff Wishbone stared at Cassidy, waiting for him to quit whining, and take his punishment. Cassidy stared back with a firm gaze for a few moments, then, as if he realized that complaining was doing no good, glanced away. With a sigh, he shuffled past Sheriff Wishbone and into his cell.

'That's more like it, Cassidy, you'll get no favours from me.'

Ignoring the mumbled oaths that he could hear Cassidy muttering to himself, Sheriff Wishbone unbolted his first cell, and more gently than before, manoeuvred Cassidy inside.

With the cell doors shut, he leant on the bars, and decided to give Cassidy the benefit of some of his collected wisdom gained while working in Redemption City.

'Bill McGruder is the worst card-cheat in Redemption City, perhaps in the whole of Kansas. So, Cassidy, you get one night in the cells for pulling a gun on him, and another night for not spotting he was a cheat earlier.'

Feeling pleased with this put-down, Sheriff Wishbone left Cassidy to stew. Once he was back in his main office he swung himself into his chair, contentedly threw his feet on his desk, leant back and, staring at the ceiling, hummed tunelessly.

Despite this poor start, Sheriff

Wishbone suddenly realized that he'd like having a deputy around after all. Especially one who made mistakes that he could enjoy putting right afterwards.

* * *

'You some kind of card-sharp?' the young, fair-haired man slumped in the corner of Cassidy's cell asked.

As Cassidy glanced at the only other occupant of Sheriff Wishbone's cells tonight, he considered his unfortunate first evening in Redemption City for a few moments. He decided that admitting he was a lawman would hardly lead to a comfortable couple of days with this young man, so he leant against the bars, and settled for avoiding the question.

'Some kind, the kind that ends up in jail.'

'Know what you mean, Cassidy.'

Although he wasn't interested in the answer in the way he guessed the young man would think he was, Cassidy asked, 'So, what are you doing in here?'

With a nervous gesture, the young man wrapped his chestnut-brown hide jacket across his chest, and laughed, his voice low and sad.

'Got into a fight in Roger's Saloon and Sheriff Wishbone gave me twenty-eight days in here.'

Cassidy nodded. Deciding to get comfortable for his stay here, he sat on the edge of one of the bunks.

'Twenty-eight days in here. To cool off. I suppose?'

'Yeah, to cool off.'

Cassidy whistled under his breath: this was an extremely tough sentence for a mere fight, and made Cassidy pleased that Sheriff Wishbone had arrived before his own altercation with Bill McGruder had spiralled further. Before too much longer, Cassidy would have been forced to spend far longer than just two nights sitting in this cell. Apparently, Sheriff Wishbone didn't stand for nonsense of any kind, but once he'd resolved this initial misunderstanding, Cassidy guessed that he'd learn to like his new boss's attitude to wrongdoers.

'You live around here?' Cassidy asked, deciding to take the opportunity to gauge the criminal element of Redemption City from a perspective he never usually had.

'What's it to you?' the young man snapped back.

Cassidy reconsidered his question, and decided that there was nothing sinister in asking where someone lived.

'Nothing, nothing, just making conversation. We're going to be here, stuck together, for a couple of days. Just don't want to sit here in complete silence.'

The young man slapped his thigh with one hand, and pushed himself to his feet, to walk the six paces to the cell door, then spun round to face Cassidy.

'Sorry, I'm just a bit nervous. I guess my pa ain't going to be too pleased when he discovers what I've done to end up in here.'

Cassidy nodded in sympathy. More

than twelve years had passed since Cassidy fell out with his own pa, when he'd decided to become a lawman instead of working on the family farm. Although this young man's problem was almost the complete opposite of Cassidy's, he thought he understood enough about life to know his worries would be unfounded.

Smiling, Cassidy shook his head, and said, 'Don't fret, he'll forgive you. I'm sure.'

The young man laughed in a single burst and stared at the ground.

'You don't know my pa, Brett McBain. He's the best, at everything. No one crosses him, ever. He's always done the best for me, and I never want to disappoint him. Finding me here is going to be a big disappointment to him.'

Cassidy nodded his head; his father sounded like a good man. Feeling unwilling to stop offering sage advice, Cassidy suggested, 'I still wouldn't worry. I'm sure after Brett's yelled at you a bit, he'll soon forget everything.'

While staring at the floor the young man shook his head.

'Don't rightly think so, my pa sent me on ahead, and I had a job to do before he got to Redemption City. With me in here, it don't look now as if I'm going to get it done.'

'What job was that?'

The young man opened his mouth, then shut it quickly, and waved his hand at Cassidy.

'Don't matter none, not now.'

With this dismissive comment, the young man turned away to stare at the wall, and Cassidy decided this was enough conversation for a while. Through the one barred window the light had already dropped to a murky glow, and although he knew he had no chance of sleeping just yet, Cassidy lay back on his bunk, and dragged his Stetson over his face. After getting comfortable, he closed his eyes, and hoped that life in his new home would improve tomorrow.

2

Riding hunched and morose, ten miles out of Redemption City, Brett McBain pulled the brim of his Stetson further down his forehead to shield his eyes from the setting sun. He'd hoped to finish his journey before nightfall, but with his sons, Daniel and Jason, putting more effort into complaining than riding, they hadn't made good time. They'd been riding north-west for four straight days now, the miles of prairie and scrub-filled land merging into an endless brown and green dirge. Soon, they'd return this way, except then, Brett hoped, they would be a whole lot happier than on their ride to Redemption City.

'Ah, Pa can't we stop, I'm hungry?' the eighteen-year-old Jason asked from a few yards in front of him, as he rode hunched in his dirt-streaked slicker.

'You're always hungry, Jason, you can eat when we get to Redemption City.' Somehow, despite his gawky thinness, Jason never thought of much beyond his stomach.

At his side, Daniel, who was two years older than his brother, in age if not in ability, rolled back and forth as if he were sleeping, and whined:

'We're never going to get there, and it's nearly dark.'

Brett gritted his teeth, and concentrated on staring at the mane of his bay. With luck, Nathaniel had secured a place to stay tonight, and he could grab a few hours of peace from his idiot sons before tomorrow's important business.

* * *

When they arrived at Redemption City the sun had already set and the stars were growing in brilliance against the endless sky, but none of the usual bustle that Brett expected to find at any place after sunset was taking place.

They trotted down the main road, lined with stores, hotels, and at least three churches, but entertainment was only noticeable by its absence.

'Where's the saloon, Pa?' Daniel asked.

For once Brett didn't complain about his son's unwanted question; he was wondering the same thing. His previous visit to Redemption City had been too short to notice these little details, that's why he'd sent Nathaniel on ahead to search out the important features of this town.

After a few moments, glancing up and down the main road, he noticed a saloon, half-lit and not particularly inviting. Brett pointed, dragged his horse across the road, and after securing it outside, shuffled on to the porch. At the door, he glanced up at a ragged sign, proclaiming this place was Roger's Saloon, and waited for Daniel and Jason to finish securing their horses. Looking back down the road, he glanced at the bank, nestling right on the edge of town, just as he remembered it.

Brett allowed a small smile to play on his lips. No matter how lacking in entertainment this place proved to be, the bank was the only place that interested him. Deliberately, he didn't point out the bank to his sons; they would be sure to start pointing, or in some way draw attention to their interest.

With his two sons behind him, Brett strode into the saloon to see that the only inhabitants were three poker players, who, as one, glanced up and grinned. At any other time Brett would have joined them; they appeared so bored that a night with another person would be sure to cheer them, but he had matters that were more important on his mind.

Brett strode straight to the counter and banged on the chipped wooden surface with his fist, until the barkeep shuffled from a back room.

The rosy-cheeked barkeep wiped his

hands on his yellowing apron, and beamed happily.

'Well hello, gentlemen. Come for the next revival meeting? Unfortunately, that's not until next weekend, although better come early than late, I suppose.'

Daniel and Jason snorted behind him as Brett slammed a few coins down on the counter and muttered, 'Three whiskies.'

The barkeep smiled.

'I'll take that as a no to the revival meeting, then.'

After the barkeep had poured three full glasses, Brett sipped, then swilled the stinging liquid round his mouth before swallowing to take some of the grit away.

'Tell me, barkeep, have the religious lot taken this place over totally?'

Shaking his head sadly, the barkeep said, 'They sure have. This used to be a fine town, we used to get all sorts. Prospectors from the hills in the north, cattle drovers. But now, just the revivalists.'

'Shame, seems such a promising town.'

They stood in companionable silence for a few moments, before Brett decided they had sufficient mutual understanding to ask the only question he wanted answered.

'I'm looking for my youngest boy, he came here a few days ago.'

'Seen no one new in town who looked much like you, or your sons,' the barkeep said, shaking his head.

'Doesn't look like me much, he's fair-haired.' Brett stopped his description as the barkeep had begun to nod his head furiously.

'Sounds like a lad who came in here a few days ago, shooting his mouth off, and a lot more besides. Sheriff Wishbone arrested him.'

'Pa, what're we going to do?' Daniel asked, leaning against the counter.

Brett lifted his hand, silencing Daniel, and rubbed his chin. Clearly, he now had more business here than he'd first thought.

* * *

Humming happily to himself, leaning back in his chair, Sheriff Wishbone tapped his foot gently on his desk. With his hands behind his head, he allowed his evening to pass pleasantly.

When he heard the main door fly open, he jerked his head forward. Peering from beneath his Stetson, he glared at the completely black-clad man in the doorway. The only hint of colour in his attire was the tied-down brown holster. The man was gaunt, without a spare ounce of fat, and had a chiselled face and deep set eyes that spoke of past hardships.

'What can I do for you, stranger?' Sheriff Wishbone asked.

'The name's Brett, and you have my boy in your cells.'

'And?'

'I've come for him.'

Aside from Cassidy, currently the only person in his cells was a young man who'd been drunk three nights back, and had wounded another man after an argument over a woman, a local preacher's only girl. Sheriff Wishbone saw no reason to make things easy for Brett.

'What's his name?'

'Nathaniel.'

Smiling, Sheriff Wishbone clattered his feet to the ground, and said, 'Nope, got no person of that name here.'

He watched Brett champ his jaws as he ground his teeth.

'Young man, fair-haired, blue-eyed, quiet, except when drunk or riled.'

That was a fair description of the young man who'd said his name was Matthew. Tiring of the guessing game, Sheriff Wishbone nodded.

'Yup, that sounds like a man I have in my cells called Matthew, but you said his name was Nathaniel. Giving a false name when arrested is a serious offence.'

'Matthew is his middle name,' Brett snapped, stepping forward a long pace towards him.

On such a peaceful evening Sheriff Wishbone felt no need to argue his point. Proving the young man's real identity wasn't worth the effort for such a trivial offence.

'Suppose I don't care what his name is, he only wounded a man, and for that, he gets a month in the cells, to cool off.'

'Where's the man he wounded?'

Slowly, Sheriff Wishbone stared up and down at Brett, from his piercing green eyes to his low-slung holster. Sheriff Wishbone prided himself on his ability to sum people up quickly and after his brief consideration of Brett trouble was the only word that sprang to mind. Not that causing trouble would do any good; Sheriff Wishbone knew his duty, and with Brett's son behind bars, no attempt at intimidation from this man would alter anything.

Speaking softly, Sheriff Wishbone kept his gaze firmly on Brett's eyes, judging his reaction.

'The injured man's resting up in

Roger's Saloon. Doc Parson got the bullet out, and he should be on his feet soon.'

Brett nodded, his eyes narrowing slightly.

'Glad to hear it. I'll be back, soon.'

Sheriff Wishbone waited until Brett had reached one long hand towards the door before he shouted:

'Won't do no good talking to the injured man, he doesn't want to press charges.'

With a little grunt, Brett swung round.

'Then why you holding my boy?'

Smiling, Sheriff Wishbone relished his answer. He always liked letting troublemakers know immediately with whom they had to deal.

'He's still here, because *I* pressed charges, and I say, he gets a month in the cells to cool off.'

Brett opened his mouth, then slammed it shut again. Breathing audibly, Brett leant on the door for a few moments. Sheriff Wishbone could see Brett's right hand twitch a little as he slowly tapped his hip. Then, with a small nod, Brett glared at Sheriff Wishbone and muttered:

'All right, how much to let him out?'

If Sheriff Wishbone had anything else to amuse himself with, he would have kicked Brett out immediately for daring to make such an offer, but feeling in the mood to annoy someone, he asked:

'How much?'

After rocking his head from side to side for a few times, Brett said:

'Hundred dollars, for your trouble.'

As if he was weighing up this offer, Sheriff Wishbone tapped his chin, and stared at the wall, then smiled.

'Sounds good.'

Brett strolled to the desk with an easy, rolling gait, grinning all the time, reached into his inside pocket, pulled out a wad of cash, and began to count out one hundred dollars.

Sheriff Wishbone waited until the cash nestled in a little pile before him.

'Looks fine. I'll see you in twenty-five days.'

Brett grabbed the table with both hands and, leaning forward, stared into Sheriff Wishbone's eyes.

'What? I'm not paying any more than the one hundred dollars we just agreed.'

Deciding he'd humiliated this stranger enough, Sheriff Wishbone leant back in his chair, smiled, and said:

'No need. I have to feed him for a month, and one hundred dollars will do, unless you want me to feed him real fancy food. That'll cost more.'

Brett grabbed his cash and breathed slowly through his nostrils while he glared at Sheriff Wishbone. Without further comment he pushed back from the desk, strode to the door, stormed through, and slammed the door shut.

After a few moments, Sheriff Wishbone slipped to his window, and stared through to see Brett join two other young men as they strode across the road to Roger's Saloon.

Sheriff Wishbone knew without a

doubt that he'd get to see Brett again later, and equally clearly Brett's boy wouldn't leave Sheriff Wishbone's cell until another twenty-five days had passed.

★ ★ ★

Outside Roger's Saloon, Daniel shuffled in front of Brett.

'Did you get him out then, Pa?'

Brett winced, then opened his arms, looking at the ground and around his feet, as if his errant son was hiding under his coat. He stared at his confused son, his sarcasm obviously lost.

'Did you, Pa, did you?'

With a sigh, Brett shook his head, and decided to stick with the facts.

'No, not yet.'

'When you getting him out?'

As Brett shuffled into the saloon he muttered, 'As you should know: tomorrow, everything happens tomorrow.'

* * *

With the early morning sun now well into the sky, Brett stood outside Redemption City's bank and stared at Daniel and Jason. With anyone else he wouldn't have to repeat his instructions, but to be sure he grabbed each son by the shoulder, pulled them together, and waited until they stared directly at him.

'Right. Daniel, you stay outside the bank, and make sure no one comes in. Stop them in a friendly manner, but less friendly if you need to, understand?'

Daniel smiled. ''Course I do, Pa. I'm not stupid, we went over all this last night.'

Brett winced. Stupid wasn't a suitable word to describe his eldest son's lack of intelligence. Snapping his order through gritted teeth, Brett said, 'We also went over the details this morning, twice.'

With his brow furrowed, Daniel

mumbled, 'We did, did we? Anyhow, when do you want me to create the diversion?'

Brett stared at Daniel, who patted his jacket happily anticipating causing some mayhem.

'Probably not at all, everything seems pretty quiet at the moment, so we won't need a diversion.'

'Ah, Pa, you promised.'

Pressing on with his set of commands, before annoyance bettered him, Brett stared at Jason.

'You come with me, but stay back, ready to help if anybody inside reacts.'

Jason grinned. 'Sure thing, Pa, you can trust me.'

Brett hoped so. After a deep breath, he nodded at Daniel, who suddenly asked:

'What about Nathaniel? When do we rescue him?'

Brett opened his mouth to reply, then decided that explaining would be too complicated, as the answer depended on how the next few minutes went.

'Later, Daniel, later, just concentrate on one thing at a time.'

Not wishing to confuse either son with more instructions, now he'd stated their simple purpose, Brett strode into the bank. To his relief, his observations of the last hour were correct, no one else was inside, except for one smartly dressed teller.

Like most banks along the Western trail from Beaver Ridge, the building had a main room with an enclosed counter along the back wall and only one, locked, entrance on the left-hand side. Behind the counter was a door to a back office, where Brett assumed they kept the safe. The teller stood behind the glass that stretched from the counter to the ceiling, and although this could easily be broken, the noise and time taken would reduce a robber's chances of escaping easily. Brett preferred the subtler methods.

At the counter he smiled at the stern-faced teller until he received a faint smile back. Then, with a small nod, the teller asked:

'What can I do for you, sir?'

'I'd like to make a withdrawal.'

Behind him, Jason snickered. Brett gritted his teeth, hoping the teller wouldn't react. The best way to deal with this was to be as quiet as possible, preferably not make any fuss at all, especially as he still had to get Nathaniel out of jail.

'What would your name be?' the teller asked.

'Ronald Smith,' Brett said, and waited until the teller opened a thick ledger of account details. Then, keeping his eyes firmly on him, ensuring the teller wasn't registering concern, Brett slowly drew his Adams from its holster, holding the weapon just below the counter. When he was sure the teller had both hands well over the counter, far from any under-counter alarms or hidden guns he might have, Brett gently lifted the Adams up to the eye-level of the teller.

The teller flinched, then frowned at the gun.

'I'm guessing I won't need this book, after all.'

Keeping his voice low, Brett said, 'If you want to live to serve more customers, close the book real slow, then step back from the counter.'

The teller did as ordered and, without being asked, sidled with his hands above his head to the doorway to his enclosed office. To Brett's nod, he opened the door, and Brett strode inside.

'What do you want. Mr Smith?'

'Open the safe, and we'll be on our way.'

Shaking his head, the teller strode into the back office of the bank. With a quick nod to Jason, Brett followed, staying a few paces back. He doubted the teller would try anything, but he watched every movement on the assumption that he would.

At the back wall, the teller knelt on one knee beside the large safe. With a series of quick movements, the teller swirled the safe combination-lock, and threw the safe open. Standing back, he waved at the safe, and with a remarkably confident voice said:

'Be my guest, Mr Smith.'

Slightly taken aback at the ease of this robbery, Brett waved for the teller to stand back against the wall, then called to Jason.

'Everything fine out there?'

'Yeah, Pa, Daniel is doing nothing.'

Daniel doing nothing always comforted Brett, only when Daniel started doing things did disasters usually occur.

'Good, bring me the bags,' Brett snapped.

'Bags?' Jason mumbled.

Brett opened his mouth to shout 'bags', again, then glancing at Jason through the open office door, saw that his son hadn't brought the cash bags inside, as they'd previously agreed. Gripping his gun more tightly in annoyance, he glared at the teller, who gave him a slight smile and nodded to a desk beside the safe. Although the bags Brett could see on the desk were far smaller than the ones they had brought to Redemption City, Brett couldn't see that he had any choice.

Trying not to let this setback annoy him more than it already had, Brett grabbed two bags, fell to one knee and stared into the safe. To his surprise all he could see inside was one bulging bag and a small pile of bank-notes. Confused for the moment, as he hadn't expected the local lumber companies to pay their workers in gold, he grabbed the bulging bag.

Quickly he shuffled the bag open. Inside, he could only see brown dullness, with a few hints of silver. On pouring the coins on the floor, he only confirmed that the bag didn't contain gold. He stood up and kicked at the cents and dimes for a few seconds, then lunged with one hand and grabbed the teller round his neck.

'Now, Mr Teller, it would appear that you're holding out on me.'

'Holding out on what?' the teller gasped.

Brett squeezed his hand, and pushed upwards, forcing the teller to stand on tiptoe. With his other hand, he pressed his Adams against the teller's neck.

'Now, we are going to get us an understanding. You volunteer information, and as a reward, I don't shoot you.'

With his eyes boggling slightly, the teller gasped. 'What information?'

'The location of your other safe.'

The teller opened and closed his mouth rapidly, but no sound, other than a faint wheezing emerged. Realizing that he was squeezing a little too hard, Brett released his grip slightly.

With a squeaking cry, the teller gasped, his throat bulging against Brett's hand.

'What other safe?'

With this worst possible answer, Brett tightened his grip, and whispering, counted to ten. With each count, the teller's face turned through increasingly bright shades of red. Brett waited until the teller started to bang his fists against Brett's arms, before releasing all pressure. Instantly, the teller plummeted to the floor, dragging in great, racking gulps of air.

Brett stared down at the teller's prone body, gave him a few seconds to ensure he wasn't going to pass out, then tapped his boot gently against the teller's leg.

'I'll give you a few moments to think about your answer a bit more; assuming, that is, you don't fancy bleeding to death from some new holes I'm going to make in you.'

'I don't know anything,' the teller said as he rolled to his knees, still gasping for air. With one shaking hand he clawed at his necktie, loosening his collar, before staring up at Brett and mumbling, 'There is no other safe.'

'That wasn't very bright.' Brett kicked the teller in the ribs, and watched him fold around his boot, then slide back against the wall.

This new pain seemed to bring some fighting spirit to the teller, who shuffled to sit on the floor and stare defiantly up at Brett.

'I don't know what you think I have here, but all the money I have is those coins, and a few notes, fifty dollars maximum, probably a lot less. Take that if you want, but I have no more.'

Brett strode in a circle, running this information through his mind, then stared down at the teller. Abandoning subtlety, he slowly set his Adams on him, and smiled, letting the teller know that he would have no problem using the gun.

'I don't want no fifty dollars. I have it on good authority that over the next few days you pay the wages for all the local lumbermen and other businesses from here, and somehow, I don't think fifty dollars will cover that. So, where have you hid the rest of your last cash delivery?'

Without warning, the teller suddenly burst out laughing, then winced, holding his ribs. 'Ooh, that hurts, don't make me laugh.'

'Quit laughing,' Brett shouted hitting the teller across the cheek with the back of his gun hand.

The slap resounded in the small office as the teller grabbed his bloodied cheek, then he glanced at Brett, one small chuckle escaping his lips.

'From whose good authority would you have learned that piece of information?'

'I ask the questions,' Brett snapped, then tailed off. His world had just re-formed into a new shape, and not a shape of which he liked the look.

The good authority was standing outside. Obtaining the date of the last cash delivery was the only piece of information he had trusted Daniel with collecting. Unable to take his annoyance out on his son, Brett strode a long pace towards the teller. With a lunge, he grabbed him by the neck, and pulled him to his feet. He couldn't try to knock sense into his son, he didn't have enough time, but he could try doing it to the teller.

'Tell me, Mr Teller, when did you distribute the wages money?'

'Three, maybe four weeks ago,' the teller said, with a gleam in his eye that still implied he found this amusing. Brett did not.

'When is the next time?'

No longer looking so amused, the teller stared at the floor, and mumbled, 'Don't know.'

Brett smiled. Now he'd an excuse to assuage his annoyance. After flexing his fingers, he closed his long hand round the teller's neck.

'I think you do.'

The teller clawed at Brett's hand, but fingers used to counting bank-notes had no impact on Brett's iron grip. Despite his ineffectual fumbling, the teller still managed to gasp, 'Don't know.'

Brett squeezed a little more. 'Tell me.'

'All right, all right,' the teller

suddenly gasped.

'Go on,' Brett said as he relaxed his grip a little.

The teller drew in a lengthy wheeze.

'The wagon riders will deliver the next consignment of money next Tuesday, and I'll pay out the bulk of it to the local businesses over the following few days.'

Brett nodded. Behind him, he heard his son step into the office.

'How do we know he's telling the truth, Pa?' he asked.

Irritated by Jason's pointless question, Jason's failure to bring the bags, and Daniel's failure to discover the right day to raid the bank, Brett felt his heart begin to thud. He gritted his teeth, and instead of letting go of the teller's neck, as he had intended before, he squeezed his fist tighter. He kept on squeezing, hearing thudding deep in his head, as the teller gasped and floundered, batting his arms increasingly helplessly. Brett only let go when something seemed to give and the teller slumped in his grip.

With a sudden step back, Brett released his hand and the teller collapsed, boneless, to the ground. Feeling a little irritated with his burst of anger, Brett kicked at the now dead teller, then spun away.

'Look what you made me do, boy,' he muttered.

'I did nothing, Pa.'

'That's the problem,' Brett muttered under his breath.

Brett grabbed the few bank notes from the safe, stepped over the teller's body, and quickly locked the office door. With Jason a few steps behind, he stormed to the front door, and, in a reflective moment of caution, turned the bank sign to CLOSED.

As Brett opened the door, Daniel spun round to him.

'How did it go, Pa?'

Brett didn't reply, but stared down at his collected bank-notes, judging there to be twenty-five dollars; not much for a man's life.

Trotting beside him, Jason said, 'Not that well, apparently we got the wrong day.'

Daniel stuck out his bottom lip.

'How could that happen, Pa?'

With his annoyance worked out on the teller, Brett felt completely drained and now eager just to move on.

'Forget it, boy. We get Nathaniel, then we're out of here.'

'Do you want us to come with you, and help?' Daniel asked.

'No.'

'I could cause a diversion.'

'No diversion,' Brett shouted, then softer, 'just get the horses.'

Brett stared at both his boys, until they both stared at the ground. He'd had enough of their help for one day.

Showing sense for once, Daniel said, 'I'll go get the horses.'

After trusting his sons with this one simple task, Brett strode across the road to the sheriff's office, ready to put Redemption City well behind him.

3

Sheriff Wishbone hummed quietly to himself as he tapped one foot against his desk. Through the door window, he could see Brett McBain open the bank door, speak to his two sons, and then stride across the road towards him.

Out of habit, Sheriff Wishbone slipped his .45 from its holster and checked he was fully loaded. Somehow, he doubted Brett was going to accept his second refusal to let his son go quite as easily as he did yesterday.

Through his window, Sheriff Wishbone saw Brett stride on to his porch, and immediately throw his door open. Not waiting for Brett to close the door, Sheriff Wishbone asked:

'What do you want, Mr McBain?'

Brett hurled the door shut and glared at Sheriff Wishbone.

'Pardon? How do you know my

surname?' he snapped.

Sheriff Wishbone always made it his job to find out about any strangers in his town, especially the obviously non-religious newcomers.

'I've been asking around. Seems that you stayed at Roger's Saloon last night, and checked out this morning.'

Brett rubbed a hand over his chin for a few seconds, staring defiantly back at him, then his shoulders slumped slightly.

'Yeah, I'm just passing through. Saw no reason to stay here any longer, and I've no intention of coming back this way, don't fancy no divine revelation.'

Noticing that his belligerence appeared to be disappearing fast, Sheriff Wishbone nodded.

'Your choice, Mr McBain. Where should I tell your boy that you've gone, assuming you want him to follow on, when he's completely cooled off, in twenty-four days?'

Softer now, Brett said, 'If you don't mind, can *I* tell him where I'm going?'

Sheriff Wishbone stared for a few moments, trying to judge whether Brett was still rooting for a confrontation. From Brett's casual stance, he couldn't tell, but Brett's request was acceptable: family always had a right to speak with prisoners.

Having made his decision, Sheriff Wishbone nodded.

'All right, but you get no time alone with him, and you can speak to him through the bars.'

Brett pouted slightly, and glanced back out of the window for a moment.

'That's mighty sad. How am I supposed to give him a good slapping through the bars?'

On feeling some of the tension in the room fade, Sheriff Wishbone laughed. He'd stayed distrustful for so many years that even here, in the most peaceful of all towns that anyone could hope to find, he still expected violence from everyone. He should have known that nobody would try to break his son out of jail to avoid a one-month sentence.

With this thought, Sheriff Wishbone smiled, pushed himself from his chair and grabbed the cell keys.

'All right, you can go in his cell. I'll give you five minutes, just leave your gun on my desk.'

Brett unbuckled his holster, clattered it down on to Sheriff Wishbone's desk, and muttered, 'Two minutes will do. I hate goodbyes.'

'All right,' Sheriff Wishbone said, as he pushed the holster into his top drawer.

At the entrance to the cells Brett grabbed Sheriff Wishbone's arm, reached into his jacket with his other hand, and pulled out some bank-notes.

'Here, take this, about twenty-five dollars, for my boy's keep, make sure he doesn't starve.'

Sheriff Wishbone had never accepted any form of bribe in his life, but this money felt as if Brett gave it with honest intent, without wanting anything in return, so he slipped the notes into his jacket pocket.

'I'll look after him.'

As he unlocked the cell, Sheriff Wishbone stared at Cassidy, who lay on his bunk in the corner of his cell, apparently asleep. Standing in the doorway, Sheriff Wishbone wondered if he should let his deputy out now. Discipline was one thing, but he'd already made his point. A little leniency now would go a long way to forging a good working relationship. Deciding to wait until Brett had gone, Sheriff Wishbone left Brett with his son and strode back to his desk. Once there he opened his drawer and stared at the man's well-cleaned gun. Sheriff Wishbone had seen quite a few double-action Adams in the war, but not so often as of late.

Only a minute passed, without any obvious noise from the cells, before Brett returned, shaking his head.

'That was quick,' Sheriff Wishbone said.

Brett nodded. 'Yeah, as I said,

doesn't take much to say goodbye. You got children, Sheriff?'

'Nope.' Sheriff Wishbone held out Brett's holster.

As Brett slipped into the gun belt, he smiled.

'You're a wise man. When I think of the idiots I produced, I wonder why I ever bothered.'

Sheriff Wishbone watched Brett straighten his clothing, and when he had his belt properly attached, decided to offer some encouragement.

'Nathaniel doesn't appear that bad to me, bit headstrong, but I'm sure he'll turn out good, if he learns this lesson.'

'Nathaniel ain't mine, probably explains why he's so bright. I just look out for him. My other two lads are out there.' Brett nodded towards the window, and Sheriff Wishbone glanced to the road too.

Across the road, by the bank, Sheriff Wishbone could see two young men loitering aimlessly by their horses. Even from this distance they didn't appear too clever. Sheriff Wishbone opened his mouth to offer some encouragement, when from the corner of his eye, he saw Nathaniel shuffle into the doorway. Instantly, Sheriff Wishbone went for his gun, but Brett had already whirled his arm, the Adams nestling in his hand before Sheriff Wishbone had even managed to drag his .45 from his holster.

Despite his irritation, Sheriff Wishbone whistled.

'Fast.'

Brett grinned. 'You're not bad yourself, you reacted fast enough to stop pulling your gun, that sort of thing helps to keep men alive.'

Although Brett was breaking out such a minor criminal, Sheriff Wishbone hated to see anyone get away from him. While staring at the Adams pointed unwaveringly at him, Sheriff Wishbone glanced from the corner of his eye at the door to the cells, wondering if Cassidy had realized what was happening out here.

Raising his voice slightly, hoping to catch Cassidy's attention, Sheriff Wishbone asked:

'Why? I'm only keeping Nathaniel here for a month, breaking him out of jail will make him a wanted man, and now you've pulled a gun on a sheriff, you'll be a wanted man too.'

Brett grinned. 'Nice to be wanted.'

Speaking as loudly as possible now, Sheriff Wishbone slammed his fist on the desk for additional emphasis and noise.

'This is no joke. When I catch up with you, and I will, you'll both get far longer than a month in the cells to cool off.'

Brett rocked his head from side to side.

'Why did you have to start threatening me? I hate that.'

Sheriff Wishbone saw the small flash of light, and what felt like a hot fist punched him in the stomach, as the bullet ripped through his guts. Unbidden, he fell to his knees. With his teeth clenched against the pain he knew would come the second his body realised that it'd been shot, Sheriff Wishbone managed to whisper, 'Cassidy?'

'What's that you say?' Brett asked staring down at him.

With the room rapidly darkening, he heard Nathaniel shout, 'Come on, Pa, let's get going.'

Forcing himself to keep his head up, Sheriff Wishbone just managed to grab the side of his desk before the world spun and he found himself lying on the ground staring at Brett's boots. Darkness rushed towards him as the boots strode to the door.

As he heard the door slam shut he saw two more boots trot into view, and Cassidy knelt beside him. Feeling his world collapse around him, he heard his own voice, disconnected from his mind, mutter:

'Get him, Cassidy, get him.'

* * *

Kneeling on the ground, Cassidy stared down at Sheriff Wishbone, at the dark red blood bubbling from the corner of his mouth clearly showing that he didn't have much longer left. As gently as he could, Cassidy lowered him to lie flat on the ground, then stared around looking for his Peacemaker and holster. Sheriff Wishbone had taken them when Cassidy had arrived, and he had no idea where the sheriff would keep confiscated weapons.

Standing beside the desk, he frantically threw drawers open, but could see nothing inside. Without much choice, he knelt and unhooked Sheriff Wishbone's gun belt; the dying sheriff mumbled for a moment as he moved him. Then, as he dashed to the door, Cassidy wrapped the belt around his hips.

He could hear people shouting and screaming outside the office. Just as he reached for the door, someone dragged the door handle from his grasp, and he stumbled back. Unsure of the identity of the new arrival, Cassidy scrambled for the sheriff's .45, but he'd only just hooked the belt on, and he didn't reach his weapon immediately.

'Hold on there,' a voice cried. 'Touch your gun, and die.'

Cassidy stopped trying to grab his gun, and glared at the man who stood outside, recognizing the sallow face of Jake Grounding, one of last night's poker players. Just managing to keep his voice controlled, Cassidy muttered:

'Come on, hurry, they'll get away. And get the doctor, Sheriff Wishbone is dying.'

Still keeping his gun on Cassidy, Jake called over his shoulder, 'Sheriff Wishbone's been shot, but I've got the man who did it.'

With one hand Cassidy gripped the doorframe, and glared at Jake, trying with the force of his stance alone to persuade Jake to move aside.

'Hey, stop blocking my way, they're getting away.'

Jake narrowed his eyes, stepping back a half-pace.

'Your accomplices have already got away, but we'll settle for you.'

Cassidy saw George Rogers lean over Jake's shoulder, staring at Sheriff Wishbone. George pulled his own gun, and trained it on Cassidy.

'Looks like we captured a genuine outlaw, all by ourselves, perhaps we might make deputies for the new sheriff.'

After a quick glance at Sheriff Wishbone, who no longer appeared to be breathing, Cassidy stared at the ceiling. He had hoped to make sheriff soon, but not this way. Lowering his gaze, he stared at Jake and George.

'Believe you me, gentlemen, when I start recruiting deputies, you'll be the last people I'd choose.'

George tapped Jake on the shoulder. 'What's this cheating murderer on about?'

Jake shrugged. 'Beats me.'

'While you two jokers stand around

talking, they are getting away, we need to get going.' With this pronouncement, Cassidy took a firm pace forward through the door, to see Jake and George stretch their gun hands forward, whilst stepping back a short pace.

'You are going nowhere,' Jake shouted, his voice a little high-pitched.

George nodded. 'Yeah, he's right, except, that is, back to your cell.'

Cassidy stared from one man to the other, and decided that whether a bullet came from an experienced gunfighter, or these two fools, the result would probably be the same. Slowly, and with as much dignity as he could preserve, Cassidy swung round, and sauntered back to Sheriff Wishbone, who now lay completely still.

'Stay away from him, and get in a cell,' Jake shouted.

Staring down at Sheriff Wishbone, a man Cassidy didn't know, and now would never get the opportunity to know, he said, as softly as he could:

‘There’s no need for me to wait in the cells. I’ll stay here until we sort this out.’

‘You either get in the cell voluntarily, or feet first,’ George shouted, waving his gun at the door to the cells.

Deciding further arguing with Jake and George would get him nowhere, Cassidy strode back to his cell, and let them lock him back inside.

Back in his cell, and unable to think of any simple argument he could try on Jake and George to let him start chasing Brett, he stared forlornly at the wall. With luck, by the time he’d sorted out this little mess, Brett and Nathaniel wouldn’t have gone too far, and then he’d make them pay for what they’d just done.

* * *

With each passing minute, Cassidy felt his irritation grow. He knew that Nathaniel and Brett were getting further away from Redemption City, and the job of tracing them would become harder.

He heard a new collection of people talking in the office next door, their voices indistinct. Feeling as if he'd said the words too many times already, Cassidy shouted:

'We need to start chasing after Sheriff Wishbone's killer. Let me out, and we'll start searching.'

Apart from an indecipherable conversation next door. Cassidy received no response. Instead, he listened to what he assumed was the sounds of someone dragging Sheriff Wishbone outside, followed by complete silence as they left him to stew on his own.

When Marshal Devine had offered him this position in Redemption City, Cassidy had been unenthusiastic. The lack of people in the town, other than at the frequent revival meetings, didn't hold out much hope for action, but he'd decided that the quiet life would do for a while. With this in mind, he doubted that the good citizens of

Redemption City would be up to organizing a posse on their own to go in search of Sheriff Wishbone's killer. Worse, even if they were, he doubted that it'd be well organized.

After two hours of irritated waiting, he heard the sheriff's door fly open. Cassidy threw himself to his feet, waiting to give his visitors a hint of how inept they were. As soon as they opened the door to the cells, Cassidy rattled the bars.

'About time. Do you idiots realize how far you can travel in two hours? We need to get going.'

A smartly dressed man whom he didn't recognize shuffled close to his cell with his gun brandished, although his hand was shaking wildly.

'Just checking that you don't need anything,' said this individual.

Ignoring that he'd already stated this point repeatedly, but unable to think of anything else to say other than to repeat the simple facts, Cassidy gripped the bars, and muttered:

'I do need something. I keep on telling you. I need to get out of here, and begin to chase after Sheriff Wishbone's killer.'

'Don't have the authority to do that,' the smartly dressed man said, stepping back against the wall.

'Then who does have the authority?'

'That'll be Mayor Digby.'

Cassidy sighed. At least now he'd managed to hear a few words of sense. Keeping his voice steady, he slowly said:

'All right, get me Mayor Digby.'

The smartly dressed man shook his head.

'Mayor Digby will be busy right now. Anything more?'

Although Cassidy could think of dozens of requirements in order to organize chasing after Brett McBain, he doubted this man would be able to understand, or help. Pushing himself from the bars, he mumbled, 'No, leave me.'

'Then keep quiet; all that shouting

while we took Sheriff Wishbone away wasn't dignified.'

Cassidy lay on his bunk, leant against the wall, and muttered to himself: I'll do far more than shout at the likes of you when I get out of here.

As soon as his unhelpful visitor had closed the door to the cells, Cassidy threw himself from his bunk, trotted to the cell door, and began to run his hands down the bars. Kneeling down, he stared at the cell lock close to, and nodded to himself, with a minor decision made.

Having worked as a deputy for some years, and being in charge of many prisoners, he knew a number of tricks. Perhaps now was the time to use a few of them. He couldn't stay here for an indefinite period, waiting until Mayor Digby gave him permission to chase after Brett, so this meant he had to leave without permission.

Sheriff Quincy, Cassidy's first boss, had taught Cassidy most of what he knew as a deputy. Sheriff Quincy's abiding principle was that you couldn't hope to get the better of outlaws unless you understood everything about them. So, ten years before Sheriff Wishbone had locked him in this cell, Sheriff Quincy had also locked him in a cell, but this time to encourage him to find a way out of his predicament. He hadn't, but once Quincy had shown him how locks worked, he had only taken a few more weeks to learn how to force the lock on the cell.

This valuable lesson had served him well during his life as a lawman, teaching him that breaking from a cell was the easy part of escape. The bigger problem always came after you'd escaped. Then, you needed to get to the outside world, and that meant going through the sheriff's office, and past whoever was on duty. Knowing this, Cassidy always ensured he was on guard at all times; he worked on the basis that the cells doors were always open, and assumed the prisoners were going to come through at any time.

As far as Cassidy could make out, listening intently by the cell door, there was nobody in the outside office, and therefore escape from the office would be possible. This meant his only problem was escape from his cell. With the right tools, this would be easily and quickly accomplished, but he didn't have the right tools, so he he'd have to make do with what he could manufacture. Shuffling back to his bunk, he ran his hands over the metal frame, searching for a weak point. None was obvious.

Giving up on being subtle, Cassidy yanked the bunk over his head and threw it at the cell door. The bunk collapsed with a satisfying crash. After a quick shake of the door, to confirm this more direct approach hadn't worked, Cassidy rummaged through the bunk debris. On the mangled struts connecting the base to the legs he found two thin bolts. With a few sharp tugs he yanked them from the frame and, after staring at them for a moment, decided they were around the right length and width.

At the door he slipped his hands through the bars, manoeuvred one of the short bolts into the keyhole, and investigated inside. His straight bolt couldn't achieve anything, as he'd expected, but after bending the end of the bolt between two struts from his bunk, he was able to get the last half-inch of the bolt into a satisfyingly angled shape.

With one eye closed, and his tongue flexed against the corner of his mouth, Cassidy wedged the fashioned key into the keyhole. Carefully, he lifted the locking mechanism inside. Smiling to himself, he pulled the now opened cell door.

'Thank you, Sheriff Quincy,' he whispered to himself, then he trotted to the door to the sheriff's office. As he'd expected, they hadn't even locked this. After locating his Peacemaker hidden at the back of the bottom drawer of Sheriff Wishbone's desk, Cassidy peered through the window, on to an empty road.

He stood a few moments, torn between leaving without explaining to anyone what he'd done, and so potentially annoying the citizens of his new town, and staying to get the town fully behind his search. As he pondered, he noticed a dark stain next to the desk, and recognized the spot where Sheriff Wishbone had died, the blood still fresh enough to glisten. This sight ended his deliberations.

Despite his desire for speed to make up for all the lost time, out of courtesy he quickly rummaged for a writing implement to leave a note for whoever found he'd escaped. But he could find nothing.

Having given up on leaving any message, he slipped through the door and stood outside on the porch for a moment. Last night, he'd left his horse outside the saloon, but his steed was no longer there; that meant he needed to commandeer another horse.

Across the road, by the bank, he could see three horses. Choosing the tallest, he walked across the road to him. He kept his gait steady and untroubled, not wishing to draw attention to himself.

Outside the bank, he patted his chosen horse, untied him, and leapt into the saddle. As he wheeled round, he saw the bank door swing open, and three people rushed on to the porch.

Cassidy glanced at the empty road, leading to the prairies beyond. He could easily gallop out of here, but when he returned, he still wanted these people's respect. Surely, he thought, not everyone here could be as unthinking as the people he'd met so far were. Leaving unnoticed was one thing, but leaving when they'd noticed him was different, so he waited until the three people faced him.

'I'm commandeering this horse to go looking for Brett McBain and his gang. I was in the adjoining room when he killed Sheriff Wishbone. I'll follow their trail while it's still fresh, and check the general direction they've gone. Assuming they haven't holed up close by, I'll be back by nightfall. Make sure you have a posse organized by then, ready to go at dawn tomorrow.' Cassidy trotted back a few paces, then remembered one further crucial request. 'And make sure you've sent a message to Beaver Ridge about what's happened here, we'll need additional help. All right?'

The first man, whom Cassidy recognized as Bill McGruder, stepped forward . . . in his hands he held a Winchester uncertainly.

'We ain't taking no instructions from the likes of you.'

'No matter what you think of me, that's what you must do!' Cassidy shouted. He waited a moment, wondering what else he could say that might help matters, but could think of nothing, so he shook his head and settled for shouting, 'Now. If you're not going to come with me and help, I can't wait any more.'

With this statement, Cassidy swung round, then felt his view of the road spin as a rifle shot echoed in his ears. The next he knew, he was lying on the ground, grit burning his cheek, a heavy object pressing down on his legs. Confused, he shook his head, and glanced down to see his horse lying on the bottom half of his body; the beast thrashed, but became increasingly weak, as pools of dark blood spread around him.

Cassidy saw a shadow pass over him and glanced up to see Bill McGruder staring down at him.

'Like I say, you ain't going nowhere.'

'You shot my horse,' Cassidy gasped, unable to believe what Bill had just done. To Cassidy, this sin was almost as bad as Brett's shooting of Sheriff Wishbone.

Bill sneered at him.

'Another crime to add to your list, stranger.'

4

After his escape, the townsfolk didn't leave Cassidy alone. Once Bill McGruder had locked him in his cell, a new man stood on the other side of the cell bars sneering down at him. Cassidy could hear voices from at least three other people in the office, talking too low for him to distinguish their conversation, even if he could care what they said.

As Bill had locked him in the same cell as he'd escaped from, Cassidy pushed his wrecked bunk into a corner, and spent the time sitting on the floor, legs drawn up to his chin. So seated, he pondered, but was unable to fully decide just how stupid his new charges were.

While waiting, the only definite matter, Cassidy decided, was that once he'd sorted out this mess, he would request the quickest transfer in the history of law enforcement. Spending even one day protecting the fools in Redemption City was one day too long.

Cassidy judged the townsfolk left him in his cell for three hours before Jake Grounding and George Rogers arrived. Immediately, he stood up, and walked to the front of the cell, ready for them to let him out.

After his guard had left from his earnest vigil, Jake shouted at Cassidy:

'You, get away from the bars, step over to the wall, and then we open up your cell.'

With Jake suddenly ordering him around, Cassidy felt his anger — which he'd only just managed to suppress for the last few hours — bubble over, and he shouted back:

'I'm not doing anything, except strangle you for sheer, relentless stupidity.'

'Why? Is that what you did to Mr Thompson?'

'Who's Mr Thompson?' Cassidy snapped.

George whispered into Jake's ear, and after nodding, Jake said:

'All right, we know that you were in this cell when your colleagues killed Mr Thompson, but his blood should be on your conscience.'

For the first time Cassidy suddenly began to realize that these people didn't believe he was a deputy. They weren't being cautious, they thought he was an outlaw.

Calming now, Cassidy began to try to see events from their point of view. Keeping his voice low, he said:

'No, wait a minute, I'm not who you think I am.'

'We'll ascertain that, in court.'

Cassidy knew there was no court in Redemption City, nor, with Sheriff Wishbone's death, could anybody here hold any form of legal meeting. The nearest court was in Beaver Ridge, a week's hard riding away, so sorting out this identity problem would take longer than he'd thought, and the chances of catching Sheriff Wishbone's killer receded with each new setback.

Shaking his head, Cassidy stared slowly between Jake and George and said, 'We can't wait that long. We have to act now.'

'And what would the likes of you suggest?'

Resisting the urge to scream that they should just let him out of here, Cassidy sighed, and rubbed a hand over his unshaven chin. If he accepted that they didn't know he was a deputy, and that his presence close to a newly dead sheriff was suspicious, then any solution would take time.

With no foolproof idea coming, Cassidy mumbled, 'I don't know, but we need to sort this out, now.'

George patted Jake on his shoulder. 'Just what we thought, follow us, and we'll sort this out.'

Bemused as to what they proposed, Cassidy waited at the wall until they opened his cell, then strode to the open cell door. He'd seize any chance to clear the mess quickly.

Jake and George backed away, and Jake shouted, 'With your hands on your head, if you don't mind.'

Shaking his head, but not wanting to irritate them, Cassidy did as they requested, and strode confidently into the main office. In the sheriff's office, more people milled around. As he waited for Jake and George to join him, he avoided meeting anyone's eye.

Cassidy expected the gathered people to look through Sheriff Wishbone's records; although Cassidy hadn't seen a spare star waiting for him, the records here must show who he was, but they didn't search at all. Instead, Jake and George seized one elbow each, and marched him through the door and along the road. Concentrating on not stumbling, Cassidy allowed them to lead him across the road, and into Roger's Saloon.

As soon as he shuffled through the doors to Roger's Saloon, Cassidy stumbled to a halt. Directly in front of him were set three tables in a row, and behind the tables sat a row of stern faces. Surrounding the tables, at least thirty people sat on every available chair. Lining one wall were a row of townsfolk sitting on the counter, and at the opposite wall a ragged double row of people stood. Cassidy didn't think he could cram more people into such a small room, and from what he'd seen of Roger's Saloon last night, he doubted it had ever been so full.

The excited sounds of conversation filling the room gradually filtered to quiet as one by one the gathered townsfolk realized that Cassidy had entered the saloon. Cassidy tried to stare confidently at close to one hundred pairs of eyes, which glared back at him, bright in the gathering dusky gloom. Taken aback for a second, Cassidy glanced over his shoulder to see that, outside, a further row of people pressed against the windows and doorway.

Bemused at this huge audience, Cassidy stepped back a couple of paces. As he shuffled back, Jake and George grabbed him from behind, with one hand on each shoulder, and half-pushed, half-dragged him into a chair set before the three tables.

Once seated, Cassidy shrugged the hands from his shoulders. He was a lawman, and didn't need anybody to hold him in place. Regaining his composure, he stared straight ahead, and waited to see what would happen next.

'What is your name?' asked a short, rounded man in a towering black hat sitting opposite him, half-way along the tables.

While staring at the man's tailored jacket, waistcoat, and obviously gold watch and chain, Cassidy listened to his heart thud. He needed to avoid this meeting getting out of control, so, setting himself comfortably in his chair, he crossed his legs, stared directly at his questioner, and said:

'More to the point, what is your name?'

'I am Mayor Digby. Now, what is your name?'

Cassidy sighed. At least now he sat before someone in authority, as opposed to the idiots he had to deal with before. Judging that confidence and assurance was the best way to deal with this misunderstanding, as opposed to the prolonged screaming and shouting that he wanted to favour Mayor Digby with, Cassidy smiled, and took a few breaths.

'I like to be called Deputy Cassidy,' he said.

With his lips pursed, Mayor Digby sneered at him.

'And Deputy would be your Christian name?'

A number of people tittered, but Cassidy ignored them. In his career as a lawman he'd faced many responses, laughter wasn't the most common, but he found it easy to deal with.

'No, Deputy is my title. Deputy

Cassidy Yates, but I like to be informal and prefer Deputy Cassidy.'

'What makes you think you can masquerade as a lawman?' Mayor Digby snapped, with his tone still low and sneering.

'No masquerade. Marshal Devine legally sworn me in, ten years ago.'

Mayor Digby sneered. 'Never heard of him, and neither have I heard of you.'

Through gritted teeth, Cassidy muttered the truth again, hoping that by repeatedly stating it, he might eventually make someone understand.

'I repeat, my name is Cassidy Yates. I'm Sheriff Wishbone's deputy, and accordingly, the deputy for Redemption City. With Sheriff Wishbone's murder, that actually means I am your acting sheriff, until such time as a more official pronouncement can be made.'

Mayor Digby glanced around the gathered throng, and after a low, false laugh, muttered:

'I somehow doubt we would ever be

happy to endorse a murderer as our sheriff.'

'I am not a murderer.'

After a slow shake of his head, Mayor Digby shuffled forward behind his table, and with his elbows upon it, stared at Cassidy.

'As you say, but I don't know you, or know about any deputy being due to come here. We've always been happy with Sheriff Wishbone. He always kept trouble away. I can't see why he'd even want another lawman to help him.'

'Sheriff Wishbone requested a deputy, two months ago. Here I am, ready to serve you, if you'll let me, instead of organizing this . . . this . . . ' Cassidy swirled his arms round the gathered crowd, trying to think of a word to describe what he saw, 'this fiasco.'

'So, you are Sheriff Wishbone's deputy, sworn to be his trusted assistant in all matters, are you?'

Hearing someone at last utter the truth, even if the condescending tone of voice didn't suggest Mayor Digby believed what he said, Cassidy stretched full length in his chair. He took the opportunity to let everyone in the saloon see his assurance, and steadily stared around the crowd, carefully making eye-contact with as many people as possible. Although the few people who did stare back did so without any of the warmth or humanity Cassidy expected from such an apparently religiously orientated town.

When he'd stared in a full arc around the room, Cassidy nodded.

'Yes, I am Sheriff Wishbone's deputy, and, as I have said, I am here to be your deputy too.'

Mayor Digby stared over Cassidy's shoulder.

'Mr Grounding, you brought the so-called deputy Cassidy here to the court?'

From behind him, Cassidy heard Jake Grounding announce, 'I did, sir.'

After nodding for a few moments, and glancing around the room, in what appeared to be a parody of Cassidy's slow stare earlier, Mayor Digby asked:

'How concerned did he sound for the state of Sheriff Wishbone's health?'

'Not at all, sir, he never asked about him.'

Cassidy glanced around the crowd, who all murmured unhappily. He knew, having seen the bullet wound in Sheriff Wishbone's chest, that he hadn't needed to waste breath confirming his new boss was dead. Cassidy had seen enough death to accept the sight of a dead colleague far faster than an ordinary citizen perhaps could. Only now did he realize just how bad that might appear to these people.

'Never asked at all,' Mayor Digby said slowly, intoning each word with deliberate care. 'Sheriff Wishbone served this town for over fifteen years, with an untarnished record, and then, on the day he dies, his deputy can't even ask about his welfare. Some deputy.'

Although Cassidy never had a chance

to know Sheriff Wishbone, he, in common with all lawmen, hated discovering that any of his colleagues had died. Cassidy never wasted time worrying about the past. Always in such situations he dealt with his grief and annoyance with action. Something these people were denying him.

Doubting that he'd be able to convey his sentiments adequately, Cassidy bowed his head for a moment. Then, unwilling to have Mayor Digby lecture him, he muttered a simpler truth.

'I've seen enough men die from gunshots to the stomach to know Sheriff Wishbone was dead.'

'Oh, really?' Mayor Digby shouted, banging his fist on the table. Then, after taking a few breaths, he continued in a quieter voice, 'Personally, I wouldn't know, I've never seen anyone die before, and I don't think anybody here has your expertise in spotting dead men so readily.'

Cassidy stared at his feet for a few moments, while everyone muttered ominously. He could see that practically anything he might say would only add to his problems as Mayor Digby twisted his words. With this in mind, he decided to stick with the simplest facts that nobody could disagree with.

He waited until the room was completely silent, then said:

'All right, we need to resolve this misunderstanding. Sheriff Wishbone requested a deputy to come here two months ago. You only need to go through his records, and you will be sure to find my name somewhere.'

'Probably on a list of wanted criminals,' someone at the back of the room shouted to a round of tittered amusement. Cassidy favoured the heckler with a glare, until he glanced away.

Mayor Digby lifted one hand, and said, 'Please, no interruptions. That is a good idea, Mr Yates, but seeing as how Sheriff Wishbone, fine upstanding citizen that he was, had a little difficulty with the written word, I strongly doubt we'll find much writing to support your claim.'

'You mean that Sheriff Wishbone couldn't read or write?' Cassidy mumbled, aghast.

After glancing up and down the row of tables, Mayor Digby whispered, in a voice that Cassidy could easily hear, 'No, he couldn't. As you would know, being his deputy.'

'I'd only just arrived,' Cassidy snapped, his irritation in this ridiculous meeting finally getting the better of him. He leant forward in his chair, and shouted, 'I never had a chance to know Sheriff Wishbone, but he sounded like a good man, one I'd have enjoyed working for. Now, let's just get this meeting over with, and together we can track down his killer before it gets fully dark and we have to wait until tomorrow.'

Mayor Digby sat with a glazed expression on his face as Cassidy's outburst ended.

'I hardly think letting you leave

Redemption City will achieve much, beyond the inevitable, terrible results we'd expect if we allowed a murderer to roam freely across the countryside, inflicting, who knows what, on other innocent people.'

'I'm not a murderer. I'm a lawman,' Cassidy shouted, returning to the central truth of his existence. 'I've never done anything wrong in my life.'

'Glad you mentioned that point,' Mayor Digby said, his voice strident and echoing in the room. 'We do have the question of what you have done, since you arrived in Redemption City. Would you be so good as to tell me and the citizens of Redemption City what you have achieved in your short time here.'

Cassidy couldn't see what Mayor Digby wanted him to say. Somehow, he was beginning to understand that nothing he could say would make a difference. Lost for anything constructive to reply, he mumbled:

'Nothing, I haven't had the chance.'

‘Nothing. You have a strange understanding of the word, nothing,’ Mayor Digby said. Then paused, to repeat his steady glance around the gathered crowd, who, to Cassidy’s disgust, leaned forward, apparently eagerly awaiting each pronouncement. ‘So, as you appear unwilling to explain yourself further, I should explain to everyone here, that, as far as we can tell, you have spent most of your time in Redemption City, sitting in one of Sheriff Wishbone’s cells. Presumably, you were cleaning it, or perhaps you find the bunks comfier in there.’

‘I was in the cells temporarily,’ Cassidy shouted over a sudden burst of laughter from the gathered crowd.

‘Temporarily, and why would that be?’

Cassidy sighed through clenched teeth, and tried to think what he could say that wouldn’t make matters worse, but unable to form any logical thought, he mumbled:

‘A misunderstanding.’

Mayor Digby leant back in his chair, and threw his hands above his head.

'Ah, another misunderstanding, was it? Mr McGruder, if you would be so kind as to address this court.'

From his position half-way along the table Bill McGruder, the card-cheat from the previous evening, threw back his chair to stand, glaring at Cassidy.

Not giving Bill time to speak, Cassidy realized what Mayor Digby had just said, and shouted:

'Court? This is no court, you have no authority to convene a court.'

'I'm the mayor. I have the right to do whatever I want in my town. Any more outbursts, and I'll have you gagged.' Mayor Digby pointed at Cassidy, seemingly daring him to say anything more.

Unwilling to suffer the indignity of gagging, Cassidy decided to stay quiet, for now.

After a few moments, Mayor Digby continued:

'Now, simple soul that I am, I would

have expected a new deputy to spend his time, on arriving in a new town, getting to know the townsfolk. I might have expected him to discuss matters of law enforcement with his sheriff, but apparently not. Mr McGruder, would you be so good as to tell the court why exactly Mr Cassidy was occupying one of Sheriff Wishbone's cells.'

'Gladly, sir,' Bill McGruder said as he strode around the tables to stand in front of Cassidy.

Somehow, staring at Bill's grinning face, Cassidy doubted his testimony would help him.

5

Holed up in the Lazy Dog Hotel in New Hope Town, twenty miles from Redemption City, Brett stared at the empty moneybags. By now, he'd have expected to be halfway to the Kansas border, already on his second horse, the first suffering from the excessive weight of these bags after they'd been filled, but nothing had gone according to plan.

He grabbed one bag, ran it through his hands, and with a brief flurry of annoyance flung it at Daniel, who lay sprawled on his bed. The bag wrapped itself around his face, and Daniel floundered as he took a couple of clawing swipes to remove it. Irritated again, Brett pushed himself to his feet, and strode to the door.

'We going out, Pa?' Jason asked.

'No, we ain't going out. I am,' Brett snapped.

'Ah, Pa, what are we supposed to do?'

Brett swirled round, wondering which of a multitude of suggestions he could offer, then settled for some supreme sarcasm.

'You stay here and guard the bags, and if anyone tries to take them away from you, you know what to do.'

Not waiting for a response, which he guessed would be inane, as all forms of sarcasm were lost on Daniel and Jason, Brett threw the door open, and headed out for a breather.

Once outside the Lazy Dog Hotel, he strolled down the road, and decided to patronize the Thirsty Cowhand, the saloon nearest to the bank. On pushing open the ranch doors, he breathed in the smell of cows, horses and sweat, allowing the tinkle of lively piano music and excited chatter to wash over him.

After the sullen, deadbeat Redemption City, the sounds of ordinary folk enjoying themselves cheered him. Feeling happier already, he strolled to the counter, lifted one boot on to the foot-rail, and waited for the barkeep to notice him.

While he waited, Brett hazarded a quick glance at the bank through the saloon window, noting the building was at least twice the size of Redemption City's bank, as he had feared.

'What you having, stranger?' the barkeep asked.

'Whiskey.' Brett threw a dollar on the counter, and leant on one elbow as he surveyed the milling scene, concentrating on projecting a calm, interested demeanour.

Over his forty years Brett had learned many skills, otherwise he'd have never stayed alive and unnoticed for so long. Since he had killed his first man at sixteen, in a sudden burst of anger over some petty argument, now long forgotten, he'd now killed ten times, the last nine all in the last decade. His tally ought to make him a marked man, with a tempting price on his head. Except he didn't have a price, as nobody had connected him with the killings he was responsible for committing. His secret was to keep his head down, not make a fuss, and allow himself to blend into the background afterwards.

Tonight, he was perfectly utilizing that skill. After shooting a sheriff, a less proficient man would now be burning a trail across Kansas, as he desperately sought escape. Every person he passed would be sure to notice his desperate flight as he left a trail that even a lawman as stupid as his sons were wouldn't fail to spot. In such a frantic state his only hope would be to kill anyone who showed too much interest. Further killings would only increase the interest in him, and before long, a well-drawn likeness would appear on road corners, and he'd find his days limited.

Brett was doing none of this; he knew that nobody would expect a guilty man to stop at the nearest town, and stand in a saloon, calmly drinking, apparently without a care. Such a policy had never failed to keep him out of trouble.

From the spill of chatter surrounding him, Brett heard someone nearby say, 'Redemption City.'

Slowly, Brett slipped along the counter, close enough to listen with a practised ear to the conversation between two men standing next to him. He heard one man, with a beard like an untamed bush, say, 'Anyhow. This gang came into Redemption City shooting up everyone, and took over the bank.'

'How many were there?' his colleague asked, pushing his small, rounded spectacles further up his nose.

'Around ten.'

Unable to stop spluttering over his drink, Brett turned his unwarranted sound into a short burst of coughing. Always he found himself surprised by how tales grew. Six months from now, he'd probably hear some later version of his pathetic attempt to rob the bank, by which time he and his two idiot sons would be a fearsome, well-organized outlaw gang of fifty or more.

'You all right, stranger?' the bearded man asked.

To cover having drawn attention to himself Brett nodded.

'Sorry, I was intending to go through Redemption City next week. From what you just said, sounds like I should give it a wide berth.'

The bearded man nodded.

'For now, that'd be best. Who knows where this gang will strike next.'

'How many you say?'

'Ten.'

A new, bald-headed man sidled into the conversation.

'I heard fifteen. They rode through Redemption City like Judgement Day itself. Sheriff Wishbone stood a brave fight, faced all fifteen down, single-handed.'

While all three of Brett's new confidants shook their heads, the spectacled man muttered:

'Stands to reason he'd be single-handed, those god-fearing folk would never help. I certainly don't think they're worth dying for.'

'You mean this outlaw gang shot and killed a sheriff?' Brett asked.

'Yup,' the spectacled man said, nodding eagerly. 'Shot him five times in the middle of the road.'

For a few moments Brett wondered why, in the stories he overheard, all outlaws always had to shoot their victims more than once. In his experience, one good shot was all it took. Feigning the required level of excited interest, Brett asked:

'Did they all escape?'

The spectacled man shook his head.

'Nope, one of the gang didn't escape. I hear Mayor Digby will be trying him by now, I hope he strings him up as a warning to the rest of his gang.'

While each member of Brett's group added his section of the tale, gradually producing the definitive, ludicrous version of events, Brett sipped his whiskey, and considered the only important thing he'd learned. Clearly, the captured member of the gang was the man Brett had seen in Nathaniel's cell. Having the authorities arrest an innocent man and possibly hang him for Brett's crime gave Brett no concern, but what did concern him was if the man wasn't convicted, especially if Nathaniel had told him any details about his family. He resolved to ask Nathaniel about this later.

'Why you heading to Redemption City?' the bald-headed man suddenly asked.

Brett returned his thoughts to the people beside him, as the bald-headed man turned to him, waiting, with apparent interest, for his answer to this question. Brett knew that this was the trickiest of all questions to answer, the innocuous ones always were; to these, the less you said the better. Say too much, and you create lies that may come back later to hurt you, avoid the question, and you run the risk of someone remembering the evasive stranger. Brett settled for his usual lie:

like the best of all lies, one with a hint of truth.

'I'm heading out west searching for some land to start a farm, far away from Apaches, wars, and all the rest.'

The bald-headed man nodded, and stared into his drink. 'Sounds fine; always wanted to get myself some land too, they say you only need to get through the first winter, and everything will be fine.'

Brett glanced at the bald-headed man's hands holding the glass; although dirty and hard, he guessed they'd never worked the land. Brett knew that getting through the first winter wasn't the problem; getting through every winter was the real problem. You could work for ten years, have a hundred head of cattle, and two hundred acres of wheat, and one bad winter, and one Apache raiding party could take it all away. The only answer was gold, enough to see you through anything, because you had enough land to employ others to work it for you.

Brett said none of this, but smiled, and settled down for a couple of hours of mindless, and hopefully unmemorable, chatter.

* * *

Back in his room, Brett stared at his three boys, who appeared well bored with their night spent in each other's company, as they should, after the mess they'd made.

'How long we staying here?' Nathaniel asked.

If Daniel or Jason had asked, he'd have yelled at them to shut up, but Nathaniel, despite his mistake at Redemption City, would understand their plans.

'I reckon three, four days, before the next cash delivery arrives here,' Brett snapped, and glanced at Daniel meaningfully. He hoped that Daniel would understand from his tone how much he was annoyed with his failed attempt to find the right day for the delivery. From

Daniel's blank return stare, he doubted this.

Nathaniel nodded his head, and rubbed his chin. Brett waited for his inevitable question, and to his surprise, he actually realized that he was interested in Nathaniel's response. His was the only own common sense that Brett encountered outside his own mind.

'Going to be tricky,' Nathaniel said slowly.

Brett smiled; this was the most honest reaction possible, an acceptance that they would try this raid in New Hope Town, because Brett wanted them to, but the word 'tricky' was a tactful understatement of their problem.

Brett had first realized earlier this summer that years of small-scale robberies had failed to get him anywhere, other than enough to live on until his next robbery. He knew that he needed to change his attitude if he didn't want to end his days face down in a ditch when, finally, he encountered someone more devious, faster on the draw, or just plain luckier than himself.

As if fate understood his desire, a chance had arrived. When travelling on the trail from Beaver Ridge, he'd seen a wagon approach from behind. A dozen serious-looking guards in short, dark blue jackets had flanked the wagon, rifles prominent, and their steady canter showed no sign of stopping, no matter who blocked their way.

With no choice, Brett had slipped from the trail, and waited for them to pass. Each guard on his side had stared at him meaningfully as they passed, seemingly assessing him for his ability to cause trouble. He had no desire to do that, just yet.

As the entourage receded into the distance, Brett had mused that such a heavily guarded wagon must contain something worth stealing, so he followed it, always maintaining an unthreatening distance. Each time that he crested a small mound, Brett stopped and stared at the wagon and the accompanying riders. He had confirmed that the wagon was an old stagecoach, with the top half sawn off. Across what would have been the seating area a metal mesh had been laid, although he couldn't see what lay underneath the mesh.

Once in Beaver Ridge, a few seemingly disinterested enquiries in the first saloon he had visited ascertained that the wagon contained wages for the local businesses, mainly railroad workers. Apparently, as many of the workers were itinerants, and left the state without spending their cash, the wagon riders regularly needed to replenish all the local banks.

Always keeping in the background, and maintaining a disinterested posture as he stared at the reflection in a shop window, Brett had watched the wagon as it halted next to the bank. There, an attentive seeming armed guard had transferred money to a set of equally attentive other guards. If the wagon itself appeared poorly constructed, then the people guarding it ensured this was a formidably safe way of transferring money.

Brett had nearly dismissed robbing this wagon, but the dogged persistence that had kept him searching for his big break for the last decade made him keep going, searching for the guards' actions. Brett knew all chains were as strong as their weakest link, and he just had to find what that was with this wagon.

For five days he had followed the wagon to each port of call; five towns, big and small, and at each the same efficient process of ensuring the money went to the right people took place. Having travelled further west than he had intended to, Brett had almost given up hope, and was wondering what to do next, when finally, at the end of the line for the wagon, his perseverance had paid off. Brett found the weak link at Redemption City, when the wagon had unloaded the last of the cash.

Unexpectedly, after the wagon riders completed the delivery to the bank, and without further fanfare or any sign of anyone collecting the cash, the wagon had turned around. Slowly, it had trundled out of Redemption City, surrounded by the wagon riders, and headed back to Beaver Ridge, presumably to begin the next round of deliveries. Brett couldn't believe what he saw. The wagon riders had guarded every other delivery so methodically, but here they showed no sign of waiting until someone collected the cash.

Afterwards he had hung around outside Redemption City for two days, watching the trail into town, as five different groups of men arrived, took their share, and left to deliver to the local rail-workers, lumbermen and other businesses.

The funds left when the wagon reached Redemption City would be far smaller than at any time on the journey across Kansas, otherwise the wagon riders wouldn't have judged returning as more important than guarding. Brett didn't mind. He only needed enough money for the rest of his life, and he guessed the contents of Redemption City's bank would achieve this. This bank was as small and as vulnerable as any bank he had ever seen.

Only then did he make his mistake. Instead of waiting for the next delivery, stealing the money on his own, and running, he decided to take his family along. He collected Jason, Daniel, and Nathaniel from down South on his uncle's old farm, and encouraged them to share in this plan.

The result of his desire to bring his family back together was that four months later they were hiding in New Hope Town, and they had no money.

Shaking his head to free his thoughts from old problems, to concentrate on the future, Brett said:

'You're right, Nathaniel, this raid will be tricky, but every chain has a weak link.'

Brett watched Nathaniel's eyes drift

over to Daniel and Jason, and Brett laughed. Now he had to hope that he could find weak links in the wagon's defences, which were even weaker than the weak links he had to carry.

Remembering the conversation in the saloon, Brett asked:

'You know that man you shared a cell with in Redemption City?'

'Cassidy?'

Brett shrugged. 'Whatever. Did you tell him anything important about yourself?'

'Why?' Nathaniel asked, furrowing his brow.

'The mayor of Redemption City thinks he's part of our gang, and arrested him for shooting Sheriff Wishbone.'

Nathaniel turned away to stare at the wall. From his hunched stance, Brett could tell that he hadn't taken to the idea of killing with the same speed that Daniel and Jason had.

'I said nothing to him, Pa,' Nathaniel mumbled.

Brett didn't press the matter further. If Nathaniel said that he'd left no clues as to their identity, then he trusted him.

After throwing himself back on to the bed, Brett stared at the ceiling, and began to run through the wagon riders' routine for transferring the cash from the wagon to the bank, to the waiting armed guard again. Somewhere in the process was the weak link, and he just had to find it.

6

Only when Cassidy saw a procession of men drag the rope, tied into a noose, from the back of the saloon, did he realize that they really were going through with this. Bill McGruder's testimony concerning his first night in Redemption City had been damning, and the account of his escape and capture, when suitably augmented, hadn't sounded too innocent either.

All through this nightmarish interrogation he had assumed that he'd just have to wait until the proper authorities arrived, before they could resolve this problem. The only thing keeping Cassidy cheerful was the collection of abuse he'd scream at Mayor Digby for subjecting him to this unnecessary ordeal.

Unbidden, his legs began to shake as he stared at the noose for long seconds.

Unable to form any rational thought, Cassidy gulped back his mounting fear, and stared at Mayor Digby, ensuring he stared directly back at him, eye to eye. In his clearest, most assured voice, Cassidy said:

'You can't do this. I'm innocent.'

Mayor Digby snorted, and glanced around the saloon. 'I haven't passed a verdict yet, or the sentence. The rope's only there in case you're guilty, and we decide to hang you.'

Desperately hanging on to the truth that a mayor of a God-fearing town such as Redemption City must surely know, Cassidy leant forward, and shouted:

'This is no court, this is no trial, and you have no jurisdiction.'

Slowly, Mayor Digby nodded his head.

'You're right. Sheriff Wishbone is the only one with jurisdiction, and as you killed him, you'll have to make do with me.'

Cassidy couldn't believe that a man

who had reached such high office could be so ignorant of the law.

'Sheriff Wishbone didn't have jurisdiction either; he wouldn't preside over the murder of a sheriff, he'd get help from Beaver Ridge.'

Mayor Digby threw his hands in the air.

'Well, we'd expect an outlaw to know all about legal matters.'

Cassidy threw himself to his feet, strode forward a pace, and shouted:

'What? When I don't know something, you say as a deputy I should know, but when I know something, you say I'm an outlaw for knowing. I don't care what you think, but there is a right way to do things, and this isn't it.'

Sneering, Mayor Digby leant back in his chair and glanced down his row of unknown accusers.

'Out here, we look after ourselves, and unless anyone wants to speak for you, I find you guilty of the murder of Sheriff Wishbone.'

Cassidy waved his arms above his

head, and shouted, 'I was in a cell when Brett McBain killed him.'

'Be quiet, Cassidy, I haven't finished. You are guilty and hanging is the punishment.'

Cassidy hung his head for a moment and said, his voice low:

'Hanging is your verdict, and that's fine. You should know that when a proper, sworn-in officer of the law arrives in Redemption City, then he will explain to you how you should go about conducting a trial. When that happens, we'll clear this mess.'

Staring at Mayor Digby, Cassidy allowed the rest of his statement to go unsaid. After clearing this mess, he would ensure that Redemption City would get a new mayor, and one who knew how to treat prisoners correctly.

'Sorry, we ain't bothered about waiting for a sworn-in, legal officer of the law,' Mayor Digby shouted. 'Because we intend to hang you tonight.'

As the terrible truth of Mayor

Digby's words resounded in Cassidy's mind, he felt Jake's and George's hands fall on his shoulders, dragging him backward to thrust him into his chair.

'Wait,' Cassidy shouted, 'you're making the worst mistake of your life.'

'I don't think so.'

With a struggling twist, Cassidy pushed himself to his feet, stepped out of the range of the grabbing hands, and stood free. He span round, desperate to find someone in this room with sufficient common sense to realize that this was wrong.

'Listen,' Cassidy shouted. 'Would you please listen to just one thing? The man who shot Sheriff Wishbone should swing for his murder, and I promise you that, despite this fiasco, I won't rest until I find him, and ensure justice. Anyone, including me, who kills a lawman, should suffer the punishment you intend to give to me, but you must do this properly. You must get in touch with Beaver Ridge, get them to send a new sheriff, and when you do, he'll confirm I am who I say I am. Surely you can wait a short while to prove you have the wrong man?'

Mayor Digby laughed.

'Don't need no proof, I have the right man.'

From behind, Cassidy felt Jake's hands grab his shoulders and, this time, he couldn't shrug them away.

'Don't, Mayor Digby. This is madness, you must have some doubt. Lock me up until a proper lawman gets here, and proves I am Cassidy Yates, your deputy.'

'When we locked you up before you escaped; don't sound like the actions of an innocent man. We don't want you escaping again.'

'You have my word that I won't escape.'

Laughter echoed around the room.

'All right,' Cassidy shouted, trying to regain some understanding. 'Guard me properly. I'm a deputy. I know how to organize guard duties; let me tell you what to do to stop me escaping.'

'Wait,' Mayor Digby shouted.

'At last,' Cassidy mumbled to himself, breathing deeply. Even with heavy hands around him, he managed to stare Mayor Digby straight in the eye.

'We forgot the other matter. I also find you guilty of assisting in the murder of our bank teller, Mr Thompson.'

'That's not even a valid crime, you don't know anything about how to conduct a trial,' Cassidy shouted, trying ineffectually to free himself from Jake's grasp.

Mayor Digby waved one hand at him.

'Now, take him away.'

George's hand reached across his face, and clamped on Cassidy's mouth. He felt himself dragged backward across the saloon. Kicking with his heels, Cassidy couldn't gain purchase on the wooden floor to try to stop Jake and George dragging him from the saloon. He clattered through the swing doors, to find himself pulled into the road.

Outside, Jake wrapped a stranglehold around his neck, and George stood at his side, pinning his hands behind his back. So held, they dragged him backward, and backward.

Before him, he could see the townsfolk pour from the saloon, with their subdued murmuring during the mock trial now freely growing to an excited clamour of indistinct shouting. Before everyone had joined him in the road, he felt a bag land on his head, new hands pulled it down over his eyes and, unable to shake it off, the world disappeared for a moment.

Locked in his own small hell, he could see, through the small gaps in the rough bag, the vague outlines of other people, as they joined the group from the saloon to form a solid crowd around him.

As the townsfolk accompanied his desperate backward journey, they waved firebrands over their heads. With his vision so curtailed, he felt himself surrounded by a swarm of angry fireflies, which shouted and screamed, the words running together into a sea of abuse.

He needed to concentrate all his effort on his staggering, stumbling, backward journey, as he tried to retain some dignity. Suddenly, George and Jake staggered to a halt, and before he could gain a firm footing to attempt to run, they lifted him from the floor, and dragged him over something that from the smell was clearly a horse.

With one leg thrown over the horse, he waited, straddled, and disorientated. He felt his arms pulled back and tied behind his back. A rough noose landed around his neck, the grating rope rubbing under his chin, as another hand pulled the rope tighter.

Then the coldness of solitude surrounded him. There were so many things that he wanted to shout out, but he'd tried every argument that he could. Everything he'd said they had thrown back at him.

Close, almost beside his ear, he could hear a new voice.

'My son, at the last, is there anything you wish to say to make your peace in this world, before you enter the next? You have that right, as do all God's children.'

Grabbing hold of his one, faint chance, Cassidy said:

'Are you a priest?'

'Of a kind,' the voice said.

Keeping his voice far more assured than he would ever have thought possible, Cassidy whispered:

'Then listen carefully. I hardly know this town, or its people, but I do know this is a God-fearing town. Surely you must be able to forgive anyone, anything.'

'I do, my son, Sheriff Wishbone was a good friend of mine, but I have already forgiven you your crime.'

Cassidy gulped. He'd said the wrong

thing. His mind wasn't working correctly. Speaking quickly, while trying to gather his thoughts, Cassidy muttered:

'I have committed no crime. You are killing the wrong man, and when you discover what you've done, you'll never be able to forgive yourself.'

'Forgiveness is absolute from God, open your heart to Him.'

'You're not listening,' Cassidy shouted, sensing the man had stepped back from him, and that his last chance had disappeared fast.

From a distance, with the voice receding, to be lost amongst the crowd's background muttering, the man said:

'And neither are you listening. Be at peace, my son.'

'Where are you? Come back,' Cassidy shouted, but he could tell the man had now gone, and he was alone. There was nothing left to do, they were going to kill him.

Realizing that his options had shrunk to nothing, Cassidy pulled in his breath, and with all his strength, screamed as loud as he could:

'Rot in hell, Redemption City!'

'Not today,' Mayor Digby shouted back, 'because today we allow one more of the devil's disciples to return to hell.'

'You may be right, but not today,' a new voice suddenly shouted, cutting across the crowd's clamour.

Cassidy strained to hear where the new voice came from, turning his head as far round as he could. Around him, everyone suddenly fell silent.

'That's good,' the voice continued. 'Everyone step away from Cassidy, keeping your hands where I can see them.'

With his head cocked to the voice, Cassidy recognized Nathaniel's voice. The son of the man who had really shot Sheriff Wishbone wouldn't have been Cassidy's first choice for a saviour, but now he'd take anyone.

With a sudden lurch he felt his horse canter forward a couple of steps.

Cassidy braced himself for the rope to pull at his neck, but the pain didn't come. Instead, he felt the noose dragged over his head, and a voice next to his ear muttered:

'Sorry, I cut that a bit fine.'

'Better than coming in another five minutes,' Cassidy gasped, gulping a few times to confirm his neck was actually free of the rope.

He felt Nathaniel cut the ropes on his arms away, and, with a shake of his head, Cassidy removed the bag. Now he could see clearly for the first time.

A sea of torches surrounded him, and he was on the edge of Redemption City, underneath an old, gnarled tree. The sight of the entire town, of about one hundred people, didn't cheer him. He tried to remember these were good people, but knew that a crowd often sank to depths that the individuals would never achieve. Although, with the burn on his neck still warming him, he didn't fancy trying to talk sensibly to them.

From the crowd, Mayor Digby stepped forward, and shouted:

'Whoever you are, we'll not rest until the both of you swing for what you've done to this town.'

Nathaniel lifted his gun, and, realizing that he was about to shoot mayor Digby, Cassidy lunged forward and pushed Nathaniel's gun downward. On seeing Nathaniel's confused look, and not wishing to push this precarious position, he mumbled:

'No time, we need to get away.'

Nathaniel nodded, swung his horse around, and with one shot into the air, which sent the whole crowd to kneel down, covering their heads, Nathaniel bolted away from the town.

Cassidy decided to follow suit, so he grabbed the reins, and forced his horse to follow. As the sea of faces blurred past him, he managed to catch the eye of Mayor Digby, and shouted:

'I'm innocent, and I'll prove it!'

The last thing he saw was Mayor Digby spitting on the ground, and then he was out of Redemption City, following Nathaniel's shape, bolting into the moonlit darkness.

7

'Slow down, Nathaniel, slow down,' Cassidy shouted.

To his relief, this time Nathaniel did slow his mad dash into the night.

'What's wrong? I suppose you're not used to night-time riding. Well, to me, this sure beats the hell out of day-time cantering.'

Normally, Cassidy might have agreed, but the near horrible death he'd just avoided hadn't put him in the frame of mind to enjoy such activities. Glancing back along the trail, now looking like a dark stream in the faint moonlight, Cassidy could see no sign of pursuit. From what he'd seen of the inept actions of the citizens of Redemption City, he doubted they'd be capable of putting together a posse.

Despite this, Cassidy knew you didn't get to live a long life by making careless mistakes, so he shuffled his horse closer to Nathaniel.

'So, what's the plan now?'

With a quick gesture, Nathaniel wiped his forehead on his sleeve and he stared back along their route.

'Well, that sort of depends on you.'

Nodding to himself, Cassidy considered. If he wasn't a deputy, he'd run, and keep running, never to return to these parts, but that wasn't an option for him. He was a lawman. Whatever happened to him, he had to put the crisis straight and that meant tracking the real killer, arresting him and, ultimately, proving Brett was the guilty party, and not himself. Although he owed Nathaniel his life, he still had to bring his father to justice. Not much of a way to repay his bravery, but he had no choice.

Unable to voice any of these thoughts, Cassidy settled for asking:

'Why did you come back for me, Nathaniel?'

'Don't really know, to be honest.'

Cassidy stared at Nathaniel, whose face was hidden beneath his Stetson in the moonlight. Not wishing to push, yet, Cassidy nodded.

'Whatever your reasons, I'm in your debt. Thank you.'

While Nathaniel stared back and forward along the trail, Cassidy gritted his teeth. He had just made a sort of promise, and he never broke promises, but being in the debt of an outlaw was sure to lead to problems when he called in that debt. Cassidy just hoped the price wasn't something that he couldn't pay, such as not arresting his father.

'Right, the way I see it,' Nathaniel said, breaking into Cassidy's pondering, 'if you want to make a run for it, we should part company here. We've been heading north for the last half-hour, and you can just carry on as far as you want. If you want to come with me, then we need to leave your horse, bury your saddle, and cover our change of direction. Then, we'll double up, and swing round back east to New Hope Town.'

Faced with these options, Cassidy only had one choice.

'New Hope Town it is.'

* * *

Forty miles out of Beaver Ridge, Marshal Douglas wrenched his horse round in a small circle to stare back along the trail to where the wagon rider's leader, Dale Furlong, pointed.

'Look over there, Marshal,' Dale said.

With his eyes shielded against the sun, Marshal Douglas could see that Dale was right, someone was following them. Closing fast, a lone rider spurted across the prairie, a small funnel of dust pluming behind him.

With a nod to Dale, Marshal Douglas dropped back, and set himself between the wagon and the new rider, ready for any action the unknown man might take. While he waited, Marshal Douglas sat tall in his saddle, a large man, greying at the temples, his trusty .45 hidden beneath his long frock coat. Although he doubted any single person would try anything, Marshal Douglas prided himself on never taking chances.

Once the rider had crested a small mound before him, the rider began to pull in the reins, and with a prancing, snorting slide, the horse came to a stop beside Marshal Douglas.

'I'm looking for Marshal Douglas,' the dust-coated rider shouted as soon as he had his horse fully under control.

'You've found him,' Marshal Douglas said, tipping his hat slightly.

The rider reached back, grabbed a saddle-bag, and threw it to Marshal Douglas.

'Got a message for you, Marshal.'

Wasting no time, Marshal Douglas opened the bag, tore open the envelope inside and quickly read the message. When he'd finished, he glanced up at the gasping dispatch rider.

'We've got water on board; you and your horse should take some before heading back to Beaver Ridge.'

The dispatch rider beamed, his smile gleaming across his dirt-streaked face.

'Thank you kindly, Marshal.'

Marshal Douglas nodded back as the dispatch rider trotted after the wagon at a far more sedate pace. Although urgent dispatches like this were not common, Marshal Douglas realized that this was the first time a dispatch rider hadn't spent the next few minutes trying to find out what the message said, usually in increasingly unsubtle ways. On the other hand, bad news travelled faster than good news, and perhaps the dispatch rider already knew the contents; there was no suggestion his message was a secret.

After joining the wagon, Marshal Douglas drew alongside Dale.

'Got some bad news for you; some outlaw tried to raid the bank at Redemption City, and killed Sheriff Wishbone.'

Dale winced.

'Sheriff Wishbone was a good man.

Have they got the killer?'

Deliberately, Marshal Douglas drew in a deep breath, and stared ahead for a few moments before replying. When he spoke, he made his statement a solemn oath.

'Not yet, but I'll find him.'

'Make sure he swings, Marshal.'

Marshal Douglas had intended to stay with the wagon all the way to New Hope Town before heading off north, but not now. He needed to get to Redemption City as quickly as possible, before the trail went colder than it had already.

'See you in Redemption City, and be careful, there's obviously a gang of bank raiders about,' Marshal Douglas called, as he urged his horse to a gallop.

Behind him, Marshal Douglas heard Dale shout:

'We're always careful.'

Marshal Douglas didn't turn around to this comment. He was already putting his previously minor duty of helping to guard the wagon behind him. Now he had something more important to deal with. Nobody would ever get away with killing a lawman, not when the authorities had assigned Marshal Douglas to the job of tracking the killer down.

* * *

With the first dawn light reddening the window, Brett awoke, and immediately noted that Nathaniel still hadn't returned. He'd heard him trying to sneak out around midnight, and, content to let the young man do whatever he wished to do, Brett had pretended to be asleep. He knew that Nathaniel was worthier of his trust than his other sons were, even after his slight mistake in Redemption City. With this trust in mind, Brett had expected him to return before dawn.

Mirroring this thought, he heard footsteps outside. With practised stealth, Brett slid his Adams from his holster, slipped off the bed on the opposite side to the door, and resting his arms on the bedside, waited to see who entered his room. Intently, he watched the door open. Nathaniel slipped inside. Behind him another man whom Brett recognized walked into the room, although Brett couldn't remember where he'd seen him.

'Don't move, stranger,' Brett said, taking no chances.

Nathaniel lifted one hand.

'It's all right, Pa, this is Cassidy.'

Now Brett recognized Cassidy as the man from Nathaniel's cell in Redemption City. Staring at Cassidy, and seeking a reaction, Brett said:

'Heard they were going to string you up.'

Nathaniel laughed.

'Not any more, I put a stop to that.'

'Well done, son,' Brett said, although he felt no pleasure in what his son had done. Complications, he could do without right now. Deciding to temper his feigned congratulations, he lowered his voice and muttered, 'But why bring him back here? We don't need to associated with a lawman's killer.'

To Brett's surprise, Cassidy didn't appear too concerned with this comment, but just smiled vaguely. Brett had expected him to react badly.

'To be honest,' Cassidy said as he sat on the edge of Brett's bed, 'I didn't think I should go too far. Every lawman west of Beaver Ridge will be looking for me by sunset tonight. The only place they wouldn't expect me to be is here, holed up twenty miles away from Redemption City. This is the best place to not draw attention to myself, and besides, I think you owe me some place to stay.'

Brett nodded. Despite his lack of enthusiasm on seeing this stranger, he liked everything he'd just heard. Cassidy had sense enough not to force a confrontation over his wrong accusation, and his request for a place to hide was reasonable but, best of all, Cassidy had assessed his situation as Brett would have done. Cassidy wasn't running, because staying calm would be safer.

With a brief nod, Brett said:

'All right, you have a place, for the next three days.'

'Why only three days?'

Brett felt no need to bring Cassidy into his plans.

'Because in three days, we're a-leaving.'

'What, now?' Jason said from the other bed. Brett hadn't realized that he'd woken.

'No, you idiot, go back to sleep,' Brett snapped.

Jason leant up on one elbow, and with his other hand pointed at Cassidy.

'Who's this man?'

'Mind your own business, and go back to sleep.'

As Jason rolled over, Cassidy shuffled to sit with his feet on Brett's bed with his back against the wall. He stretched long and hard, then smiled, and when he spoke, his voice was more assured than Brett would expect for a man who had so recently faced a lynching.

'I know what you're going to try and do here in three days' time, and you'll never do it.'

'Do what?' Jason asked.

Brett sighed, deciding to avoid asking Jason to go to sleep again. Instead, he pointedly ignored Jason, and stared at Cassidy. Trying to appear disinterested in the answer, he asked:

'How do you know what we're going to do?'

'The wagon will return on its next run soon. I assume your murder of the bank teller in Redemption City had something to do with the wagon run.'

Brett clumped to a spare chair, and dropped into it. Whilst planning this robbery he'd only taken his own counsel. Jason and Daniel couldn't be trusted to wipe their own noses, so he'd never discussed any aspects with them, and force of habit meant he only gave Nathaniel specific tasks to do. Now, with this stranger having arrived, he felt something change. At the very least, the idiot to non-idiot balance in the room had just changed to favour the non-idiots.

Keeping his gaze on Cassidy, Brett muttered:

'The teller's death was a mistake, but I'm putting that mistake down as a trial run; when the wagon arrives here, we'll attack, and this time we'll succeed.'

Staring up at the ceiling, Cassidy whispered:

'Suicide, they'll guard it too well.'

Brett nodded. 'Suicide for everybody, but not for a well-organized gang.'

Brett would have felt pleased with this boast if Daniel hadn't chosen this moment to wake up, and suddenly shout:

'What day is it?'

'Saturday,' Jason said. 'I think.'

'Oh good.' Daniel rolled over on the floor, and returned to his snoring sleep.

This display of unwatchful torpor finally decided for Brett what he should do.

'We have a plan, and a good one,

Cassidy. You're welcome to join us, and take a cut of the profits.'

Cassidy shuffled further down the bed, still staring up at the ceiling. When he responded, his voice was confident and determined.

'What's your plan?'

Staring at his hands, Brett wondered whether to tell the truth, and decided that this time the truth wouldn't harm him. If Cassidy decided not to join, he was no worse off than before.

'I'll tell you, when I have one.'

Brett saw the rim of Cassidy's hat shake as he nodded, then he threw his hands behind his neck.

'Tell you what. I've had a long night. So I'll get some sleep, and when I've had some rest, I'll see what I've thought up, perhaps add some refinements to your plans.'

With this faint sarcasm, Cassidy shuffled down the bed, pulled his hat over his eyes, and with his arms folded across his chest, began to snore. Somehow, in those last few moments,

Brett realized that his total control of this planned raid had disappeared.

To his surprise, Brett didn't feel concerned with this latest amendment; if anything, the chances of success had just grown.

8

The sun was shining down through the open window when, with a start, Cassidy awoke. Having had little sleep for two consecutive nights, he'd slept soundly for some hours into the day. Happily, he noted, he was alone. This at least gave him time to think what to do next.

Having become one of Brett McBain's gang, with little effort, he now had to work out how to turn the tables, and bring Brett to justice. However, though he thought of doing this, no plan appeared foolproof. Going to Sheriff Vermont, New Hope Town's lawman, wasn't something he fancied doing. Yesterday, he'd have gone to him without compunction, but he didn't want to risk this town using the same misjudged summary justice that Redemption City had employed.

Throughout his career, Cassidy had always put his trust in the law; now, far away from his normal patch, he no longer trusted that wearing the badge would ensure truth. He needed something safer, and that had to include capturing Brett McBain and taking him to the proper and completely trustworthy law at Beaver Ridge. To do that, he needed Brett's utter trust and confidence before springing a trap, and however Cassidy looked at his predicament, that must mean continuing to pretend he was interested in robbing New Hope Town's bank.

This left Cassidy three days to come up with a way to devise and spring that trap.

* * *

Two hours after he had woken, Cassidy forced himself to smile at Brett as the outlaw strode into the hotel room. Having forced himself to become accustomed to talking with Sheriff

Wishbone's killer earlier, Cassidy could now concentrate on maintaining his deception, without spending every moment searching for a mistake on Brett's part so that he could arrest him.

Brett nodded to him. 'You're awake at last.'

'Sure am, don't often get a comfy bed.' This was true, although Cassidy never enjoyed soft beds; he had just been exhausted.

Cassidy watched Brett throw a package down on his bed, and, opening it, Cassidy was pleased to discover a hunk of bread and some cheese. Suddenly realizing that it had been some time since he had last eaten; Cassidy quickly wolfed down a mouthful of the bread.

'I've just heard an odd rumour about you,' Brett said.

Worried about what this rumour might be, Cassidy mimed having a mouth far fuller than it was, to give him time to think. The only odd rumour possible must be that he was a lawman.

Everything else must be normal rumour. After emptying his mouth, with a pronounced gulp, Cassidy said:

'Don't suppose you get many deputies helping out on bank raids.'

Brett narrowed his eyes, his hand noticeably twitching closer to his leg.

'What?'

Cassidy laughed, and shook his head.

'Not a real lawman, of course. I told Mayor Digby in Redemption City that I was a lawman, while I tried to find a way to escape, I couldn't have been too convincing, they still tried to hang me.'

Slowly, Brett shook his head.

'That wasn't the rumour I'd heard, but I'd choose more convincing lies. When I saw you, you were in jail; you don't get many deputies on that side of the bars.'

'As I said, I was desperate,' Cassidy said, then ripped off another lump of bread with his teeth. As absolutely nobody appeared to believe he was on the right side of the law, he just hoped that when he finally did need the right people to believe him, they would.

'Anyhow, this rumour I heard was that after a fair and honest trial, you escaped from jail in Redemption City by picking the lock of your cell.'

Cassidy pondered this information while he chewed another mouthful. The only good thing to come out of this disaster was that he hadn't wasted time defending the people of Redemption City. Those people had a strange idea of right and wrong. Desperate enough to kill the first suspect they found, and not even honest enough to admit they'd tried to hang him. Their only nod to the truth was to explain his escape by the method he had tried to use.

Taking the opportunity of this admission, Cassidy smiled, and decided to offer a small lie to add to the rumoured truth.

'I think they didn't want to admit they authorized a lynching, and having heard about my exploits elsewhere, created that lie.'

'What exploits would they be?'

Thinking quickly, Cassidy decided against inventing wilder lies that, if embroidered too much, would be sure to have a flaw. He settled for giving himself the chance to prove his skills through action rather than words.

'When one of your boys returns, I'll have him get me a few things. I'll show you what my skill is, and how it'll help us get into the bank.'

'What're you planning?'

Cassidy smiled. 'Later, when I have my tools.'

With this offer, Cassidy slipped back on the bed and, while he rubbed his still sore neck, stared at the ceiling. He hoped Brett wouldn't push this suggestion too much more; he had no idea what his plan was, he'd only just thought of using his lock-picking skills. Without doubt, these skills could be useful to get into a bank; what was less clear was how they would help to trap Brett and prove his own innocence.

* * *

Three days after arriving in New Hope Town, Cassidy shuffled down inside the new set of buckskins that Nathaniel had bought him and strode purposefully across the road. These clothes were his first new ones in two years, so new they scratched across the shoulders and down his legs, but they removed any chance of someone recognizing him from the descriptions that must already be circulating.

If he were a proper member of Brett's gang of outlaws, he'd have stayed put in the Lazy Dog Hotel. With a double mission: to look like he was trying to rob the bank, and find a way to arrest Brett, he had to start to investigate New Hope Town a little more.

With the wagon due tomorrow, Brett had allowed him outside with Nathaniel without any complaint. With three days of talk failing to develop any foolproof plans, even with Cassidy's abilities to break locks quietly and quickly, Brett had appeared eager to let them both examine the bank. With luck, he and

Nathaniel might find any potential weaknesses in the bank that Brett had missed. Cassidy intended to ensure they found nothing that would help them, but he hoped to find something that would help his own plans.

As they passed a couple of shops down the road from the bank, Nathaniel slapped him across the chest and pointed at a notice-board on the wall. For a few moments, Cassidy didn't realize what he looked at; there was just a display of the usual wanted men, and then he noticed the new, darker-coloured addition.

WANTED FOR THE MURDER OF SHERIFF WISHBONE, the new sign said, NAME UNKNOWN, MAY POSE AS A DEPUTY, REWARD, DEAD OR ALIVE, $500.

'Five hundred dollars,' Nathaniel gasped.

Any other time, Cassidy might have found this amusing. The reward was miserly in anyone's language, and for the killer of a lawman, a near insult. What was more ridiculous was the artist's portrait above the offer. Cassidy felt no nerves at all while standing right next to what was supposed to be his own picture. No one would guess that this dark-haired, square-jawed, stubble-bearded man was supposed to be himself. Evil, squinting eyes stared out of the picture without warmth or compassion, and the hat was at a jaunty angle that Cassidy never used.

Cassidy made a mental note that once he'd sorted this problem out, he'd pay a little more attention to whoever drew these pictures. Perhaps he might catch a few more outlaws with a little more accuracy in the supposedly helpful pictures.

Smiling to himself, and feeling far more confident, Cassidy strolled to the bank and immediately walked inside. He stayed a few paces behind Nathaniel, who turned to Cassidy and whispered:

'Be careful, that picture was a good likeness. You're a marked man now.'

Shaking his head in bewilderment,

Cassidy rubbed his chin and, just to be sure, quickly ensured his hat was perpendicular.

While making sure he caught nobody's eyes, Cassidy stood at the back of the bank, and watched Nathaniel stride to the nearest teller, and chat to him. Apparently, Brett had deposited fifty dollars last week, and had been withdrawing a little each day, so as to examine the bank from the inside.

Taking the opportunity to look around too, Cassidy stared at the rows of tellers, five in all, sitting behind glass with a small gap at the bottom through which to pass cash back and forth. Beside the counters, he could see the closed entrance. He'd seen this same design in Beaver Ridge, and presumed it to be a standard one.

Behind the tellers was another door, which would lead to a back office and a safe. As always, the protection for the people and cash was limited, the only real effect of the doors and glass would be to slow down any raiders, and give everybody else sufficient time to organize a counter-attack. The problem Cassidy faced now was how to overcome this minuscule level of physical protection at precisely the time that the bank was also at its most manually protected.

Cassidy shook himself, and stared at his feet, feeling bemused. For a few moments, he'd completely forgotten his duty. He wasn't an outlaw looking to rob a bank, but a lawman working out how to ensure a bank raid failed, with the minimum of injuries, and clearing his name at the same time.

With his real task again at the front of his mind, he concentrated on staring at the closed door behind the tellers. The perfect place to spring any action would be in there. Trap everyone in a lockable room, and ensure the innocent parties were elsewhere.

While he considered his strategy, a new man, bulky and travel-dirty, clad in a short, dark-blue jacket, strode into the bank. Without preamble the new entrant shouted, with his echoing voice rudely halting Cassidy's thoughts:

'The name's Dale Furlong, and now is the time for you all to get out.'

For a second, Cassidy wondered whether someone else was raiding the bank, and so destroying their own raiding plans, but then Cassidy recognized the distinctive jacket of the wagon riders which he'd heard of from Brett over the last few days.

'Why? I've a withdrawal to make,' the man behind Nathaniel shouted.

'You can do that in half an hour. We're about to make a deposit,' Dale Furlong said as he stood, one leg out, rifle butt leaning against his thigh, suggesting his order was not open to debate.

Nathaniel strode across the bank to Cassidy, patted him on the shoulder, and muttered, 'Better get back to my pa, quick.'

Although Cassidy didn't recognize the wagon rider, he did his best to avoid catching his eye as he left the bank. Outside, there were no other wagon riders about, but he assumed the wagon would be here at any moment.

He glanced at Nathaniel, and trying to appear annoyed, mumbled, 'They came early, wonder why?'

Nathaniel shook his head as he strode towards the Lazy Dog Hotel.

'No idea, did you see anything in there that might help?'

'No, I was only in there for a few minutes. Anyhow, we can't worry about that now, maybe we can do this raid on another run, when we might have thought up some proper plan. At least we'll get the chance to watch their delivery procedure too, perhaps we'll spot some flaw in what they do.'

'Yeah,' Nathaniel said, his shaking voice not implying he actually agreed with Cassidy. 'But I reckon that Pa is going to be annoyed.'

Cassidy nodded. 'You're right, but he's going to have to stay annoyed, the wagon riders will have delivered the money in a few minutes time.'

'Too right, and we can't organize a raid in a few minutes.'

Feeling pleased as Nathaniel agreed with him, Cassidy glanced back at the bank. Soon the town would be full of lawmen, all from far outside this area, and independent of any desires of the locals for summary justice. He needed to get a message to one of the wagon riders, and let them know what had happened. He had no doubt they'd see sense, and not try to lynch him. Then, his only problem was to ensure he captured Brett safely, without dragging anyone else into the fight. The final question was whether he could achieve that more easily in the hotel room, or outside on the main road.

While Cassidy pondered his plan, he listened to a group of horses as they trundled into town, and glanced over his shoulder to see that they dragged a heavy wagon behind them. This was his first sight of the wagon, and the wagon riders, and they appeared as determined as Brett had said. Standing by the Lazy Dog Hotel entrance, he stared at a dozen men, identically dressed in hard-worn Levis and dark-blue jackets. This set of bulky men rode in a well-spaced, confident way that showed they owned the road as they flanked the wagon with their rifles already brandished. With much hollering, the wagon slowed to a halt beside the bank.

He smiled to himself. At least now, all thoughts of raiding the bank would leave Brett's mind. Without a plan in place, and without time to produce such a plan, added to the far superior man-and gun-power, it meant that they'd definitely missed their chance. Determinedly turning his thoughts to his new plans for trapping Brett, he followed Nathaniel up the stairs.

At their room, Nathaniel threw the door open, and without preamble, shouted, 'The wagon's here, Pa.'

'I wondered what all that noise was,' Brett shouted, and dashed to the window. 'Damn.'

'What's up, Pa?' Jason whined from a chair.

'Don't you listen, the wagon's here,' Brett shouted staring through the window.

Cassidy slowly closed the door behind him, and tried to judge if this was the right time to make his move. With everyone distracted, he could arrest them now. He decided against this action, as he needed to get word out to the wagon riders first, and ensure that Brett and his gang didn't escape if something went wrong.

'We'd better be getting out of here,' Daniel said.

Cassidy winced. This was the last thing he wanted them to do. In this hotel room he could control events, but outside in the open country anything could happen.

Quickly, Cassidy said, 'No, they'll spot us, we need to lie low here for a while, until we can make a run for it.'

Brett swirled round to Cassidy,

checked his Adams, spun the barrel, and thrust it back in his holster.

'No reason to lie low. Time to get going.'

Confused, Cassidy held out his hands. 'But they might recognize us.'

Brett rubbed his hands quickly down his jacket and smiled.

'No one knows us, and I doubt anyone will recognize you. The only thing they'll recognize is their cash disappearing into the distance.'

'What?'

Jason and Daniel sniggered as Brett strode to the door, and even Nathaniel laughed.

'You still with us, or are you too scared to go for it?' Brett asked, staring at Cassidy at the door.

Taken aback by Brett's attitude, Cassidy gasped, 'You mean you're still going through with this raid?'

'Sure am, no use waiting until the wagon is gone.'

'Have you looked outside?' Cassidy shouted, aghast at the stupidity of

Brett's intentions, despite his desire for this raid to fail. 'There's at least a dozen of the wagon riders here. They have more guns than we do, and they're well organized. We haven't a chance.'

Brett grinned. 'Probably not, but we're going in anyway.'

With this, Brett surged through the door, closely followed by the rest of his family. Feeling that events were now moving faster than he could control, Cassidy dashed after them.

9

Sitting at the front of a cart, outside Monty's General Store, Cassidy stared at the bank on the opposite side of the road. Beside him sat Jason, staring at the ground, appearing as glum as Cassidy felt. In the early afternoon few people were about, making Cassidy feel even more conscious of his position. Nothing about the situation felt right, even his new Colt Peacemaker, identical to his own, felt somehow wrong as he nervously ensured the weapon wasn't tangled in his jacket.

On the way down from their hotel room none of Brett's family had explained what the plan for the raid would be, and Cassidy couldn't muster the enthusiasm to ask. The wagon riders were sure to foil this raid, and Cassidy only needed to follow their lead, completing Brett's misguided actions.

Over the last few days, as far as Cassidy could tell, Brett's gang hadn't decided on a plan, but presumably they had made some decision when Cassidy wasn't about, or perhaps before he arrived. Although unsure of the exact details, Cassidy could guess what would happen. He and Jason had a cart, and would draw alongside the wagon as the wagon riders unloaded the bags of cash. Presumably Brett would start the raid then, and they'd just need to trust to luck that nothing went wrong.

Cassidy hated trusting to luck, and in this case this policy was sure to lead to disaster. The key for him now was to ensure that the disaster was for Brett.

Cassidy could see Dale Furlong framed in the bank doorway, standing poised, glancing from inside the building to the outside. Another wagon rider had entered the bank a few minutes ago, presumably to check the inside was secure. Outside the bank the remaining wagon riders flanked the wagon in a solid circle. If Brett hoped they might slip up and give them an opening, then Cassidy doubted this raid would last more than a few seconds.

Glancing from the corner of his eye across the road, Cassidy could see Nathaniel and Brett, who sat on their horses beside a supplies store, one hundred yards from the bank, leaning close to each other, talking animatedly. Neither appeared to be paying attention to the bank, so at least they were carrying out one part of this plan with a little skill.

Being unable to locate Daniel, Cassidy leant towards Jason and muttered, 'Where's Daniel? I can't see him.'

Jason gibbered for a few seconds.

'Don't you worry, you'll sure as hell hear him in a few moments.'

Cassidy decided not to ask what this comment meant. The raid had no chance of success, so as a lawman his only duty was to protect the innocent passers-by and his colleagues, the wagon riders. For a few moments he stared openly at the wagon riders, beginning to feel the strange last few days drift away, as he allowed himself to fully remember who and what he was.

Suddenly, with a little yank, Jason encouraged their horses to shuffle forward, and after a few increasingly louder requests, they began to trot forward. Staring straight ahead, Cassidy saw another cart trundling towards them, on the other side of the wagon, and recognized Daniel heading the cart.

Although not particularly interested in the answer, Cassidy asked, 'Which one of us is escaping with the cash?'

'We are.'

Cassidy smiled to himself. He'd never heard Jason sound so confident, and, in this situation, it was all misplaced.

Jason kept the cart trundling forward parallel to the side of the road on the opposite side to the bank, while Daniel approached them down the centre of the road. Taking the opportunity of the cart's lurching over a hole in the ground, Cassidy glanced back. Behind him, he could see that Brett and Nathaniel had dragged their horses away from the shop and into the centre of the road and followed them, thirty yards back.

Suddenly Cassidy saw an unexpected movement, and, glancing around, identified a small object flying across towards the side of the road. He only had time to realize that Daniel had thrown the object, and that the object was a stick of dynamite, before, with a deafening roar and a clattering of windows, the entire front of the shop beside Daniel exploded. Cassidy shielded his eyes as Jason yelled at his horses to surge forward.

Through the swirling smoke, Cassidy could see Daniel urging his horses to dash from the explosion. He glanced at the shop to realize that, thankfully, no one had stood close on that side of the road, or the result would have been instantly fatal.

Along the length of the road people were screaming and dashing in all directions. Some ran towards the shop, some ran away. The wagon riders did neither, but their horses were edging them away from the spreading smoke, and two horses at the back of the wagon were bucking their riders almost to the point of dislodging them. If Daniel expected the explosion to create total confusion amongst the wagon riders, the result wasn't as bad as he probably hoped.

Then, almost seeing the movement in slow, dream-like intensity, he saw Daniel pull his arm back, and launch a second stick of dynamite. This time the stick whirled in the opposite direction, towards the wagon. Unable to do anything other than shout a warning. Cassidy threw himself to his feet, and screamed the first obvious thing he could think of.

'Dynamite. It's dynamite. Run.'

To his surprise, Jason echoed his cry, and shouted, 'Watch out!'

The dynamite hit the ground a few feet back from the wagon, and fizzing and turning, rolled beneath the wagon and out of sight.

This time the wagon riders did react. The three wagon riders standing on the side of the wagon threw themselves to the ground to roll away. Those on horseback galloped away. Cassidy saw two of them rip off their blue jackets and throw them beneath the wagon, as if they were trying to smother the dynamite.

Coming out of his shock, Cassidy lurched to his left and tried to grab the reins from Jason, who still kept his steady trot forward parallel to the wagon. Jason pulled the reins away from Cassidy's clawing grasp and with a little extra speed, redirected the cart towards the wagon.

'Are you mad?' Cassidy screamed at Jason. 'The dynamite's going to explode in a few seconds.'

'The one under the wagon won't,' Jason said smiling, then, lifting one finger, he counted for a few seconds. 'But this one will.'

From beside the bank another explosion ripped through another shop. This time Cassidy was unsure if anyone was close to the latest explosion. He stared at Daniel, now forty yards away, and swinging towards the wagon, wondering if from this range he could kill him before Daniel hurled any more dynamite. Then he realized that his chance had gone and that the real raid had started as, from behind him, Brett and Nathaniel splayed a burst of gunfire across the wagon.

Thankfully, all shots missed the scurrying wagon riders, who were still trying to locate the dynamite under the wagon and to push passers-by out of the way. Jason spurred his horses on, and within seconds the cart had halved the distance to the wagon. Ahead, he could see Daniel leap from his cart on to the wagon, now temporarily unguarded.

On deciding that he'd spent enough

time as an outlaw, Cassidy grabbed his Peacemaker, and in one fluid motion aimed and fired at Daniel. Firing whilst riding a horse is always difficult, but when you're not controlling your motion at all, and the target is shrouded in smoke, the shot is doubly difficult. Not surprisingly, Cassidy's two shots failed to hit Daniel, although he must have been close as Daniel glanced up, staring around to see who had fired at him.

Having decided to wait until he came closer before shooting at Daniel again, Cassidy glanced over his shoulder to see that the wagon riders had quickly organized themselves. They had dragged their horses into a row across the road, directly in front of Brett and Nathaniel.

Listening to the volleys of gunfire from the wagon riders, Cassidy felt more assured that the slim chance of this raid succeeding had disappeared.

Confident now, and twenty yards from the wagon, Cassidy steadied his

Peacemaker, ready to take Daniel and Jason into custody. Then, without warning something hit him on the side of the head. He waved his arms as he felt hands grab his shoulder and spin him round.

In a futile gesture, he tried to duck as he realized someone had leapt on to their cart, and was trying to drag him to the ground. Floundering, he tried to push his assailant away, and stared for a second into the wide-open eyes of a densely bearded man, before the man gained a firm arm-lock around Cassidy's neck.

Cassidy threw himself to his feet, dragging the bearded man forward, then threw himself backward, and with an explosive cry landed in the back of the cart with the bearded man underneath him.

Lying on his back, he felt the bearded man's strangle-hold pull away. Cassidy rolled from him, to find that the cart had lurched away from the wagon. Quickly, he stared over his shoulder to see that Daniel had abandoned the wagon and was dashing across the road to a spare horse. As expected, this raid had failed.

After checking that his assailant was out cold, Cassidy set his feet wide in the cart, and tried to judge whom he could arrest. Unfortunately, Daniel was disappearing in one direction down the road and, glancing over his shoulder, he could see Brett and Nathaniel heading off in the other, their horses kicking vast plumes of dirt behind them. Several wagon riders peeled off from their solid row to chase after them.

Feeling resigned to the increasing disaster all around him Cassidy shuffled into his seat beside Jason, and shouted, 'So. What's the great plan now?'

'We head that a-way,' Jason said, apparently having failed to notice that Cassidy had shot at Daniel previously. He pointed at the receding figure of Daniel, now galloping out of New Hope Town. Unable to effect a clean arrest, or do anything that the wagon riders, now receding behind him, would correctly interpret, Cassidy shuffled down on his seat, and waited to see how much worse things could get.

To his surprise, they made it all the way to the edge of New Hope Town before he could see three wagon riders begin their pursuit behind him.

He leant towards Jason.

'Three of them behind us.'

Jason nodded to his right. Looking in the same direction, Cassidy noted Brett and Nathaniel arcing around the back of New Hope Town to return to their trail, closely followed by four more wagon riders.

'And those four make six,' Jason said.

'Seven,' Cassidy mumbled, but the numbers didn't matter. They were unlikely to get away, and Cassidy doubted he'd be able to explain to his pursuers who he really was in this mad dash.

Looking over his shoulder, Cassidy could see the wagon riders closing on them. He nudged Jason who, after a quick glance himself, screamed, 'Go, go.'

'We got to do something, this cart will never outrun them,' Cassidy muttered, resigned to the impossibility of explaining his actions, but at least happy that Brett and his gang were unlikely to escape now. His only fear was that if Brett escaped, the man was devious enough to evade capture, perhaps indefinitely.

'Go, go, go,' Jason shouted, cracking the reins in a futile gesture to get more speed.

From behind Cassidy heard a shot. He flinched, then glancing around saw that Brett had pulled alongside the cart and fired at them. Confused for a second, Cassidy floundered as he pulled his Peacemaker, but then realized Brett wasn't aiming at him and Jason, but at the back of the cart.

Leaning back, he saw that the man with the dense beard whom Cassidy had knocked out back in New Hope Town had stirred, and had dragged himself along the cart towards the front. Another shot crashed into the side of the cart, just feet away from the bearded man. However good a shot Brett was, shooting sideways whilst speeding flat out wasn't an easy shot to make.

At his side, Jason had noticed the bearded man too now, and he whirled round to stare at Cassidy. Quickly deciding that until he could capture this entire gang, he was better off trying to ensure that the whole gang escaped, Cassidy patted Jason on the shoulder, and shouted:

'Get ready to ditch the cart. When I give the word, get on the horses, I'll take care of him.'

Jason nodded, and without time to check he'd fully understood his instructions, Cassidy spun to his knees and vaulted into the back of the cart. Cassidy hoped Brett would guess what he was doing; he also hoped Brett would guess wrong.

With one hand on his head, the

bearded man crouched by the side of the cart, keeping his head below the wood rim as he tried futilely to protect his body from the gunfire.

After a quick glance at the wagon riders behind, who were still out of target range, Cassidy steadied himself. Then he staggered a few paces in trying to keep his balance before leaping at the bearded man.

Without warning, the bearded man threw himself at Cassidy, hitting him squarely in the midriff with one shoulder as he wrapped his arms around Cassidy's back. They both tumbled to the floor, where they rolled twice to crash into the back of the cart. Cassidy braced himself for the bone-cracking fall to the ground, but the back of the cart held.

Shaken up by the bearded man's actions, Cassidy blinked his eyes rapidly, trying to regain his balance. When clear vision returned, he found the bearded man kneeling on his chest, his fist raised ready to drive it down at his unprotected head.

'Stop!' Cassidy shouted, as the bearded man's fist thrust down at him. Cassidy threw his arm up for the fist to glance off his arm and thrust into his chest.

Grunting with annoyance, the bearded man tried to wrap his hands around Cassidy's neck, but Cassidy managed to force both arms into the air, and grabbed one hand as it closed around his wrist. Then, clawing round, he gripped the bearded man's other hand, the man's fingernails brushing against Cassidy's cheek as he pulled the hand away.

For brief seconds Cassidy struggled to push the bearded man away, then the man shifted his weight and began to bear down on him. Inch by inch his hands began to close on Cassidy's neck.

Realizing that the bearded man had the superior strength, Cassidy gritted his teeth and, trying to catch the man's fevered eyes, hissed, 'Listen.'

The bearded man grunted, pressing his knees deeper into Cassidy's guts.

Pressing ahead, although the bearded man showed no sign of listening, Cassidy gasped:

'Listen. You need to get a message to the rest of the wagon riders. I'm a deputy, from Redemption City. I've hooked up with this gang to try and stop the bank raids.'

The bearded man laughed with his face so close a spray of spittle showered Cassidy's face. Then the cart lurched and for a second Cassidy felt as though he was without weight. Then the bearded man crashed down on him, so heavily he thought he'd burst. Then the weight lifted.

Gasping, Cassidy rolled to his side to see that the lurch of the cart had thrown the bearded man feet away. Desperately, Cassidy threw himself at the bearded man's back, gripping an arm around his neck in a perfect stranglehold.

More comfortable now, Cassidy put

his mouth close to the bearded man's ear and whispered:

'Right. Listen this time. I'm not going to kill you. When I've finished explaining, you leap off the cart. If you remember to roll, you'll be fine. Once you get back with the wagon riders, just give them this message. I'm Deputy Cassidy. I'm trying to stop this gang, so if we get away, I'll pretend to work with them. I'll make sure the next raid fails, and we can capture all of them. All right?'

The bearded man struggled for a second, then relaxed, and mumbled, 'All right, whatever you say.'

Still keeping his arm around the bearded man's neck, Cassidy shuffled to his feet, then he heard an explosion of gunfire rip across the cart. He swung back to see the wagon riders now only yards away.

Without time for further niceties, Cassidy swung the bearded man at the side of the cart, for him to fall over the side, then threw himself to the front, tottering over the side to land beside Jason.

'You ready?' Cassidy shouted.

'Ready for what?' Jason shouted back as he cracked his reins.

'To release the horses.'

'Are we doing that?'

Without time to argue, Cassidy tottered to his feet, stared at the right-hand horse, and leapt just as a bullet blasted behind him.

He judged his leap perfectly, and landed square on the horse's back. The horse somehow managed to buck, despite the weight of the cart.

Wheeling his arms dangerously, and just keeping his balance, Cassidy felt himself thrown forward, his face burying itself in the horse's mane. Spitting furiously, he pulled himself back, and hazarded a glance sideways to see the other horse veering away from him.

Noting that Jason must have finally understood and released the horses, Cassidy concentrated on self preservation. He looped one hand under the bridle and, gripping with his thighs as hard as he could, did his best to twist the bridle, to steer the horse to the left to follow Brett.

To his left he could hear more gunfire, and could see Brett firing over his shoulder at the wagon riders, who were now pulling back, obviously setting in for a long chase.

Riding bareback, Cassidy swung round in a long arc, and prepared to run from justice, again.

10

Brett stared at his small fire, where the flames licked at the gathered branches, generating considerable heat, but the warmth did nothing to cheer him. In their quickly organized escape, all their meagre supplies had been in the back of the cart, now ten miles back along the trail.

Lacking energy or enthusiasm, Brett couldn't even be bothered to catch anything to eat, so they sat beside a rocky outcrop watching the sun set behind the distant hills in a reddening splash of swirling clouds. Forlornly, they passed round the stale half-loaf of bread that Jason had found at the bottom of his saddle-bag.

Although Brett hadn't expected to escape from the wagon riders, they'd abandoned their chase only a few miles out of New Hope Town. Brett guessed that they didn't want to leave their wagon with minimal protection for too long, and so had returned to New Hope Town, in case the McBain raid had only been part of a bigger diversion.

Feeling the need to fill the silence with some conversation, Brett shuffled on the ground, trying to get his position more comfy, and said, 'Well, that didn't go according to plan.'

Cassidy coughed loudly, and possibly deliberately.

'You mean, you actually had a plan.'

Brett could accept criticism from his boys, but not from this man that he didn't even know. He stared at Cassidy, and with his voice low, asked, 'What do you mean?'

'Charging up to the wagon, shooting and a-hollering, with Daniel hurling dynamite indiscriminately, hardly justifies the word plan.'

In a different time and place Brett might have agreed, but he didn't feel in an agreeable mood right now.

‘Seemed like a plan to me.’

‘What?’ Cassidy shouted, leaning forward to stare across the fire at him. ‘You said that you only had to find the weak link in the wagon riders’ procedures, and exploit it. I can’t argue with that idea, it’s sensible and might even have led to success, if you had found the weak link; but what did you think you’d achieve with that madness?’

Although Brett tried to foster some annoyance to force a confrontation, he couldn’t muster the enthusiasm. All of Cassidy’s criticism was justifiable, but he’d never expected to succeed.

‘We achieved one thing.’

‘And what would that be?’

Brett smiled at Cassidy. ‘At least we now know that such a plan won’t work.’

‘Could’ve told you that beforehand, if you’d given me the full details.’

Steadily Brett lifted his hat, smoothed his hair down, and then poked at the fire. The plan they’d just used was their first idea for the raid, devised some months ago, for them to use if nothing more sophisticated came to mind. As nothing had, he'd fallen back to it.

After a few moments' thought he decided to tell Cassidy the truth, the real reason he'd decided to go ahead with a plan that he knew had little chance of success. So, he glanced up from the fire.

'Better to die trying, than live the rest of your life wondering if the plan would have worked.'

Cassidy threw his arms over his head, and gave a short, snorting cry.

'I joined up with you because I thought we could combine our talents, not just follow your mad desire to get yourself killed.'

This time Brett felt the old flurry of anger that'd got him into so much trouble over the years, rumble deep in his guts.

'There was nothing mad about that plan, we nearly made it, everyone did as told, we just weren't lucky.'

Brett glanced at Jason and Daniel, amazed that, for once, he actually felt proud of them. Neither had made a mistake, that was something he'd never thought possible.

Daniel grinned at him. 'Did we do well, Pa?'

For possibly the first time in his life, Brett said, 'Yes, you did well.'

Jason smiled and leant over to Daniel to slap him on the back, and receive a slap on the back in return from Daniel, who shouted, 'We did well.'

'You did not do well,' Cassidy grumbled.

Daniel whirled round to him.

'You what? Pa said I did well. You can't say anything else.'

'Where did you get the dynamite from?'

'Around.'

'Are you trained in using it?'

'Might be.'

Cassidy threw his arms above his head. ' 'Course you're not, anyone who knows anything about dynamite wouldn't throw it around like that.'

Brett watched Daniel stare at the

ground, having seemingly used up his quota of objections. Brett knew that Cassidy was right; wild use of dynamite was foolish, but as this part of the raiding plan was Daniel's only contribution, he hadn't wanted to dissuade him, whatever the danger.

Guessing that Cassidy was being squeamish in his concern, Brett said, 'Leave him alone, Cassidy, nobody was hurt by the dynamite, he threw it away from any people that were about.'

'That isn't the point,' Cassidy shouted at him, then turned back to Daniel. 'Are you a gambling man, Daniel?'

'Not really,' Daniel mumbled, as he stared at the ground. Brett could sympathize, as usually a telling off from Brett consisted of a barked order to shut up. Daniel wouldn't be used to prolonged interrogation of his failings, as Brett never had the will power to explore them fully.

' 'Course you're a gambling man,' Cassidy shouted, leaning forward towards Daniel. 'Because if you explode dynamite like that . . . every time you use it, when you don't know what you're doing, you're taking a dozen gambles, and one day you'll lose, and anyone within spitting distance will be coated in bits of you.'

Brett lifted one hand. 'All right, you made your point, but I gave him permission to use the dynamite.'

'Bad decision,' Cassidy hissed.

'Are you challenging me?' Brett snapped.

' 'Course not, just bring me into your plans, especially the bits that can get us killed.'

Brett considered this statement for any hint of confrontation, but could detect none. He grabbed another unburned branch, and furiously poked at the fire, sending sparks rippling into the increasingly star-filled sky. He would have let this go, except that Jason had suddenly cottoned on to this discussion — as usual, a few minutes after it had ended.

'You saying that my pa is stupid?'

Brett watched Cassidy open his mouth, then close it and shake his head as he leant back against a rock. Brett guessed he'd been about to offer a thorough summary of just who were the stupid ones around here, but had thought better of it.

'No, I'm just disappointed; thought that raid might set me up.'

'Sounds like you're saying my pa is stupid. No one says my pa is stupid and gets away with it, because my pa ain't stupid.'

Irritated, Brett threw the branch into the fire.

'Jason, he isn't saying I'm stupid, now leave it.'

As Jason drew his blanket around his shoulders, mumbling under his breath about stupidity, Brett stared at Daniel, hoping he wouldn't follow his brother's lead by joining in, but he didn't. Daniel stared at the flames, transfixed. Under normal circumstances, this meant he'd forgotten what everyone was discussing.

Talking did seem to confuse him, before too long.

To Brett's surprise, Nathaniel piped up.

'What would you have done then, Cassidy, if you're so clever?'

Cassidy stared at the flames, rubbing his chin, not answering for long moments. When he spoke, his voice was low and measured, as if he read aloud.

'To successfully defeat the organized forces of a proficient team of lawmen you need a number of features. You need superior numbers, superior planning, luck, and opportunity.'

Nathaniel nodded.

'All that sounds fine.'

Cassidy shook his head.

'Sorry, that may sound fine, except we don't have the numbers, the planning was dismal, we had no luck, and the time we chose was wrong.'

For a few moments Brett ran those comments around in his mind. They didn't sound original or argumentative.

'Like Nathaniel says, what would you have done?'

'Nothing,' Cassidy said, immediately.

'Nothing don't seem like a plan to me.'

'Nothing is a plan when you choose to do nothing.'

Suddenly, Daniel spoke up. 'If doing nothing is a big plan, I vote we put Jason in charge, he's the best at doing nothing around here.'

Brett waved his hand at Daniel. 'Shut up, Daniel. What do you mean?'

'We needed to pick our time, not the time that was best for the wagon riders. Plan and organize, pick our moment, and generate a little diversion so all their attention isn't on the job, and *not* a diversion with dynamite. That's all.'

'I reckon,' Daniel said slowly, 'that the reason we failed was that we didn't use enough dynamite; we need a bigger diversion, not a better one.'

Brett smiled at this epic speech from his son, but decided to ignore him, and try to find out what Cassidy was considering.

'I'll buy all that, but when would be the best time for us?'

'When they're least expecting a raid. Out here, away from the main cities, the wagon-riders watch everyone and everybody, expecting someone to try a raid, but back at Beaver Ridge they'd never expect an attack. That's where we should hole up. Then, on next month's wagon run, we attack on all sides.'

'Next month!' Brett shouted. For the last decade he'd searched for the perfect opportunity; always expecting it'd be just around the corner, yet never finding it. Now, he could see the first promising opportunity he'd found, receding fast. 'Next month will be too late. After this raid, and with Sheriff Wishbone dead, they'll double the wagon riders, and any chance will have gone, for ever. We do it now, or never do it.'

After a silent few moments, Cassidy whispered, 'The companies from round about will have distributed the money they left at New Hope Town by now. We can't do nothing about that.'

Brett stared at the flames, and for the first time, the fire began to warm him. Previously, he had had no idea what to do, but Cassidy had helped to decide what he should do next. Action was the answer. Confident now, Brett said:

'Sure can't, but there's still Redemption City. The wagon riders will deliver to there tomorrow, and we'll be waiting.'

'We can't go to Redemption City,' Cassidy said, glancing around at Jason and Daniel, who immediately perked up, sitting straight and eager.

'Why not?' Nathaniel asked, before Brett could ask the same question.

'After Brett killed Sheriff Wishbone, we hardly left there as the most popular men in Kansas; everybody will recognize us. We have no hope.'

Brett didn't answer immediately, and, to his delight, Nathaniel said:

'I don't think so, you said you should

choose your moment, and strike where they least expect an attack.'

Brett laughed. 'Nathaniel is right, and I'm betting that's Redemption City, tomorrow.'

'Why?' Cassidy snapped back.

Brett returned to the only thought that'd occupied his mind for the last few months.

'When I was in Redemption City some months ago, the wagon riders didn't even stay to guard their money.'

Cassidy snorted. 'And you think the wagon riders will leave the money unguarded this time, with a bunch of outlaws at large, trying to rob banks?'

Brett smiled at Cassidy's comment. The wagon riders having left was something he had hardly believed at the time. He was prepared to accept that this might have been a one-off event, but knew that if he didn't check he would never rest easy again.

Without too much confidence, Brett said, 'No, you're right, the wagon riders will stay this time, but we'll catch them off guard, because they'll just not expect the next raid to be so quick.'

'Hope so,' Cassidy mumbled as he leant back against his rock. He stared at the ground for a few moments, and when he looked up, he no longer looked so concerned. 'Except, this time, we need to plan properly beforehand, and use my skills, instead of Daniel's explosive interests.'

Leaning closer to the fire, Brett smiled.

'Go on, I'm listening.'

* * *

Dave Bowman stared at the ceiling. Disorientated for a second, he leant on one elbow, trying to get up. Then, as the room spun even more, he instantly regretted the action and fell back to the bed, groaning.

As Dave groaned, a man strode to his side and frowned down at him.

'The name's Marshal Douglas, and you're back in New Hope Town, in the

Thirsty Cowhand.'

'What happened?'

'What happened was that you were a brave, responsible citizen trying to stop a bank raid. I'm authorized by the state to deputize you after the event. Is that all right?'

Dave still felt confused. He rubbed his dense beard and tried to make sense of what he'd just heard. Despite his confusion, he knew that he didn't want no deputizing. Determinedly, he shook his head.

'I'm hardly deputy material, Marshal,' he mumbled.

From above, Marshal Douglas smiled.

'Maybe not, but you acted when you should have.'

Suddenly, the reason he lay here hit him. He'd been wandering around aimlessly beside the bank when someone had started firing guns and explosions had gone off all around him. Facing a desperate situation, he had attacked someone in a cart, trying to drag him off so he could escape. Only when the cart had dashed from the town did he realize that the cart contained the actual bank raiders. After an ineffectual fight, he'd leapt to safety.

His embarrassment at Marshal Douglas's misinterpreting his actions taking over from his previous reluctance to be deputized, Dave mumbled:

'It was nothing. If I'm all patched up I ought to get going.'

'You sure you don't want to be a retrospective deputy?'

Dave couldn't imagine any job he wanted less, retrospective or not.

'I'm sure.'

Marshal Douglas lifted one hand, and smiled.

'The pay's twenty dollars.'

With this unexpected offer, Dave licked his lips. Twenty dollars would buy quite a few enjoyable evenings.

'Twenty dollars, you say?'

'Plus five dollars for your injuries.'

With the payment reaching such

heady heights, Dave nodded eagerly, all his misgivings forgotten. He stared at his hand as Marshal Douglas started to count the money out to him.

While Dave watched his hand fill with dollar bills, he remembered some of the things the man in the back of the cart had shouted at him. Dave slowly nodded to himself, thinking what further financial gain he might obtain for this information.

When he had the full twenty-five dollars, Dave wrapped his hand around the notes.

'How much more for information about the gang?' he asked.

Immediately, Marshal Douglas snapped back, 'Nothing, as a legally sworn-in deputy your duties include telling me everything you know.'

Dave pouted. 'Don't know nothing then.'

Marshal Douglas nodded, and spun away.

'Be seeing you, Mr Bowman.'

A momentary pang of conscience hit

Dave, and he shouted: 'Wait.'

Marshal Douglas spun round. 'What?'

Under the Marshal's firm gaze, something of which Dave had been on the receiving end from countless lawmen over the years, the pang filtered away.

'Nothing, nothing, just be careful. Those men are dangerous.'

* * *

Marshal Douglas slowly lowered himself from his horse, giving himself time to take in the lie of the new town. To him, Redemption City appeared much like any town this far into the west of Kansas except, this time, a lawman had died here.

As soon as he stood beside his horse, a florid-faced man hurried across the road towards him, his short legs pounding the ground in his haste to reach Douglas.

'Marshal, are we glad to see you, we

just don't know what to do,' the man shouted.

Marshal Douglas stared down at the small man, who straightened his towering hat as he gazed up at him.

'And who might you be?'

'Mayor Digby, at your service, and we are a town without the proper law. Who knows what types might just take hold — you hear terrible things.'

'You do at that,' Marshal Douglas said, nodding. He didn't add that in his time as a lawman he'd seen some terrible things too. Deciding that relaxing the mayor wasn't as important as getting the search for Sheriff Wishbone's killer under way, he set his hands on his hips and said, 'I'll need to see everyone who saw the man who shot Sheriff Wishbone.'

'No trouble, Marshal, I reckon we can all do that.' Mayor Digby glanced up and down the main road, where Marshal Douglas could see the townsfolk beginning to venture out from the shops to stare at him.

'You mean the whole town saw him?'

'Nope, only afterwards, when we caught him,' Mayor Digby babbled, rubbing his hands together frantically.

This was news to Marshal Douglas.

'You mean that you've caught him? The message said he was at large.'

'He is now, he escaped. We don't know how to keep outlaws prisoner, we're a law-abiding, God-fearing town. Not cut out for his type.'

Marshal Douglas glanced at Sheriff Wishbone's old office, seeing a small window with bars. With a cell in town, even the most incompetent group of people ought to be able to keep an outlaw imprisoned for a few days. He kept these thoughts to himself.

'I saw that you had a likeness posted in New Hope Town, and a reward.'

'We all respected Sheriff Wishbone. The whole town pledged to that reward.'

'Thank you kindly. Any hint of who the outlaw might be?'

Mayor Digby shook his head.

'Nothing that might be the truth. He claimed to be Sheriff Wishbone's deputy, of all things, but we knew who he was all right. Ran off with Brett McBain and his boy, after they'd robbed the bank.'

Feeling a number of details about this shooting and the bank raid in New Hope Town pull together, Marshal Douglas asked:

'Did you get a name?'

'Claimed to be called Cassidy Yates.'

Without asking for further details, Marshal Douglas grunted to himself, and strode to Sheriff Wishbone's office. He could hear Mayor Digby chasing after him, but he ignored the mayor. If there was one subject Marshal Douglas didn't want to talk about, then it was about a lawman who had abandoned his duty and gone bad.

He glanced to the west; the sun was already setting. Tonight he had some thinking to do, before he began to organize a manhunt.

11

On emerging from the scrubby prairie, Cassidy kept his head as close to the ground as possible, and sprinted for the back of Redemption City's bank. Once there, he leant against the wall and waved for Brett and the others to follow. He gulped back the slight acrid taste caused by running fast across open ground while doubled up. As he waited, he stared at the half moon, now some way up from the horizon; this meant they only had a couple of hours before dawn. If anything, that was too much time, but arriving later would mean running the chance of somebody spotting them in the growing light.

When everyone had lined up next to the wall behind him, Cassidy began a steady shuffle round the bank, always keeping his back pressed as close to the wall as possible. Thankfully, Brett's idiot sons didn't do anything foolish and, as agreed, once they'd reached the road front, Cassidy went on alone.

Under the cover of the porch above the bank door Cassidy felt confident that nobody could see him, although the protection meant he had no light to work with at all. He paused for a moment, staring at the collection of shops and churches that comprised Redemption City, a place which, only a few days ago, Cassidy had sworn never to revisit. He could see no sign of life in the town, although in Sheriff Wishbone's office, opposite the bank, he could see a solitary light. Cassidy stared at this light for a few moments, then decided to ignore it; they wouldn't have been able to recruit a new sheriff this quickly.

Putting his thoughts back on the matter at hand, and working as carefully as possible, he reached in his pocket, withdrew his shortest manufactured key, slipped it in the door-lock, and listened for the tell-tale click.

Having fashioned these keys in the hotel room as something to do to fill in his hours, he was still unsure whether they would work. He had no doubt he could create a passable key. But, during all the time he'd tried to produce them, he'd felt himself torn between producing a good key, and wanting to produce an inadequate key to ensure that the raid failed.

After a few moments of tentative delving, he found the catch inside the lock with his first deep probing; with a small clink the door swung open a few inches. Shaking his head in wonderment at the success of his first illegal lock-picking, Cassidy slipped along the side of the wall, and gave a short, low whistle, telling the others to follow. Once they'd joined Cassidy on the porch they shuffled into the bank.

Inside, he wasted no time on picking the office-door lock, and within minutes all five of them had installed themselves safely behind the counter.

'Told you I'd get you inside,' Cassidy

said easily, sounding proud of his success.

Brett nodded to him, then waved at Nathaniel.

'You, hide in the corner below the counter. Cassidy, get to the other end of the counter. I'll take the middle.'

'What'll we do, Pa?' Daniel asked.

Cassidy watched Brett take a few deep breaths.

'As we agreed last night, you will create the diversion when the wagon riders unload the cash from the wagon.'

'Carefully,' Cassidy muttered. He had only reluctantly stopped arguing against Daniel's exploding more dynamite. Despite his deep hatred of the people of Redemption City, he still had no desire to see them blown up, or, for that matter, Daniel either.

Brett grabbed Daniel's sleeve.

'Yeah, as Cassidy said, carefully.'

'Don't worry, Pa,' Jason said. 'Nothing can go wrong. I'll be with him.'

'And that's what worries me the most,' Brett said, pointing at the door.

'Shall I tell Pa about my new plan, Jason?'

Jason shook his head. 'No, let's get going.'

With a lightning lunge, Brett grabbed Daniel's shoulder and spun him round.

'And what new plan would that be?'

'Nothing really, I just figured that to create a really big explosion I could strap a number of sticks of dynamite together.'

'You figured that out all by yourself, did you?'

'I did at that, Pa.'

Brett turned to Cassidy, with his eyebrows raised. Normally, Cassidy would have suggested extra caution, but doubted that anything he could say would stop Daniel.

Cassidy whispered, 'We need to take positions before the townsfolk wake up, and stay out of range of Sheriff Wishbone's office. Someone is in there.'

Brett patted Daniel on the shoulder, and whispered, 'You heard him. Get moving, and be careful.'

Daniel nodded and shuffled with Jason to the door, where he nudged Jason and said:

'Say, how many sticks do you think we can strap together?'

Cassidy didn't hear the answer as they wandered from the bank. As soon as they'd gone Cassidy locked all the doors behind him, and took his position in the corner, behind the counter.

All they had to do now was wait.

* * *

Dawn had long since broken when they heard the lock in the bank's door turn.

'At last,' Nathaniel mumbled to a chorus of whispered hushing from both Cassidy and Brett.

Hiding behind the counter, Cassidy heard someone patter into the room, whistling under his breath. Cassidy glanced at Brett, who waved both his hands palms down, signifying he should do nothing. They waited while the newcomer shuffled back and forth carrying out whatever business a bank teller needed to do before opening up the bank for the day.

After a good five minutes had passed, with still no sign of the teller approaching the counter, Cassidy glanced at Brett, who was gritting his teeth, rubbing his Adams up and down his leg. Cassidy could see that if the teller didn't come into the office soon, he would soon be dead.

Just as Cassidy judged Brett couldn't wait any longer, he heard the office door swing open. Brett took a long swinging stride towards the man.

'Good morning, Mr Teller.'

The teller squeaked before Brett wrapped a hand over his mouth and dragged him to the floor.

'Cassidy, lock the door. Make sure no one comes in. Nathaniel, you stay out here.'

Cassidy did as ordered, and they all moved into the back office, leaving Nathaniel sitting below the counter.

Inside the back office, Brett slowly

lifted his hand from the teller's mouth.

'Right,' he said, 'this is how it'll work. You do what I tell you to do, and you live. Don't do what I tell you to do, and you die. Understand?'

The teller nodded.

'Don't kill me, mister, I've only just started this job after someone killed the previous teller. Please don't do anything.'

'The other thing that'll keep you alive is stopping babbling,' Brett snapped.

The teller gulped a couple of times, and after hazarding a nervous glance at Cassidy, mumbled, 'All right. What do I do?'

Brett smiled, and slowly stepped away from the teller to lean against the wall. 'Nothing, yet. Think you can manage that?'

Nodding furiously, the teller squeaked, 'Sure can.'

With the first part of their plan complete, they waited for the second part to materialize. Cassidy just hoped the wagon riders wouldn't be long in coming; he doubted that a whole town would be happy with the bank remaining closed all day; they would suspect that something was wrong.

* * *

Although every minute passed with supreme slowness, Cassidy was surprised that over an hour passed without incident. Then he heard a tapping at the bank door.

'Someone at the door,' Nathaniel whispered unnecessarily from under the counter.

'What you reckon?' Brett asked, staring at Cassidy.

'Ignore the first customer, but we'll have to take the second one in, or somebody is going to get suspicious.'

Brett nodded and, kneeling on the ground, well out of sight of the customer outside, shook his head at Nathaniel.

Cassidy had never prayed, but he offered a little hope to the world outside that the citizens of Redemption City would not wish to visit their bank today. The fewer people who were about, the easier it would be to stop any innocent people from dying.

To his annoyance the second customer arrived five minutes later, and began a steady, insistent tapping on the front door. Brett stared at Cassidy, who nodded back. Keeping the bank closed would raise more suspicions with the potential customers than having a nervous teller serving them.

'All right, teller,' Brett said. 'You open up, and then serve this customer. You get rid of him without any messing about. If you want him to live as well, you offer no hints we're here at all, understand?'

The teller nodded. Cassidy judged he wouldn't be foolish enough to do anything; the bigger danger here was having too many people about when the wagon actually arrived.

Once the teller opened the bank door, Cassidy heard someone ask:

'Why are you closed?'
'Sorry,' the teller squeaked, then after coughing, continued more confidently. 'I didn't know I was closed, I'm still getting used to things around here.'
'I understand the problem, takes some getting used to, I suppose. Mr Thompson served here for nearly ten years, did you know that?'
'You don't need to tell me,' the teller grumbled as he walked back to the counter.
'He never had a hint of trouble, then we get a bank raid. In Redemption City of all places.'
'And you don't need to tell me that, either.'
'Why are you closed?' a second voice asked. Cassidy glanced at Brett, who glared back at him. Obviously, the chances of completing this raid before too many people arrived had now gone.
'Apparently, he forgot to open up,' the first customer said.
The second customer laughed. 'My oh my, we didn't use to have this

problem when Mr Thompson was in charge.'

'Do you know you were closed?' a third voice asked. With this comment, Cassidy slid down the wall, matching Brett's position.

Now they had to hope the wagon would arrive later than they had expected, when the citizens of Redemption City had tired of visiting their bank.

* * *

'All right, the name's Dale Furlong, and now is the time for you to go,' a new voice shouted, breaking into Cassidy's half-snoozing reverie. He glanced at Brett who was already alert and sidling towards the office door. Carefully, Cassidy slid along the ground, and stood on the opposite side of the door to Brett.

'I said, all out. *Now,*' Dale shouted, louder this time. Outside, grumbling people filled the bank, jostling with those who were leaving.

When quiet had descended, Cassidy heard Dale stride to the counter.

'I don't know you,' he shouted to the cowering teller.

'I'm new,' the teller said. 'Bank raiders shot Mr Thompson last week.'

'Yeah, we had them try their luck at New Hope Town yesterday. Soon saw them off, the most pathetic bunch of outlaws I've ever seen.'

Cassidy glanced at Brett, who sneered, obviously marking Dale as someone who would pay for that insult.

'That's good, let's hope you keep us safe today,' the teller muttered, his voice a little high-pitched.

'That's as maybe, but I still don't know you, no one told me of a change in plan. Stay there, and don't move a muscle.'

Leaning against the wall, Cassidy darted a glance at Brett, who smiled and waved his hands palms downward in a calming gesture. This level of care wasn't unexpected.

With no choice, they waited. After a few minutes Cassidy heard the bank door open again, and Dale's voice.

'Marshal, I don't recognize this here teller. He says he's new, but I don't know nothing about no new teller.'

'Marshal?' Brett mouthed, and Cassidy shrugged his shoulders. A marshal would definitely investigate the shooting of a sheriff, but he hadn't expected one to arrive so quickly.

'I only got here late yesterday. I've hardly had a chance to get to know anyone. I'll go get Mayor Digby, check this out.'

Cassidy nodded to himself, recognizing Marshal Douglas's voice. If he was an outlaw, now he'd start to worry; Marshal Douglas was a careful and efficient lawman, but, as a lawman himself, Cassidy felt himself relax, as any doubt that he'd be able to prove his innocence eroded.

Noticing that Brett glared at him, Cassidy forced a glum expression on to his face.

'Don't worry,' he mouthed.

After a few minutes, Cassidy heard a new person enter the bank.

'This is ridiculous,' a voice said, 'dragging me all the way over here just to identify a bank teller. Yes, that is Mr Johnson. Now, can I go?'

Cassidy gritted his teeth as he recognized Mayor Digby's voice. The mayor was one man whom he'd hoped that he wouldn't have to meet on returning to Redemption City.

'No, we still need you,' Marshal Douglas said.

'Why?' Mayor Digby shouted.

'Because without your sheriff we need you to authorize the cash to be left here.'

'You have got to be kidding, there's no such rule,' Mayor Digby whined.

After his past dealings with this man, Cassidy smiled to himself to hear Marshal Douglas give the mayor orders. Cassidy resolved to add to Mayor Digby's woes when this was over; this small telling off would be nothing when compared to what Cassidy would inflict on him.

Marshal Douglas grunted.

'There might not be such a rule, but there is now.'

After lengthy mumbled complaining the mayor stayed, and Cassidy heard him clatter across the room. Cassidy didn't know what that little argument had been about, but he guessed that Mayor Digby had already managed to annoy Marshal Douglas.

Although he knew that he shouldn't think in such terms, Cassidy felt pleased that however the forthcoming gunfight panned out, if the crossfire caught Mayor Digby, then the loss to Redemption City wouldn't be too great.

After a few moments of uncomfortable silence they heard the trundling sound of the wagon's approach. Brett nodded to Cassidy. To succeed they only needed to pick the right moment to attack the wagon.

Cassidy just had to pick the right moment to attack Brett.

12

Outside the bank, Cassidy could hear much whispered conversation, then Dale Furlong shouted through the bank door.

'Right. Let's get this over with as fast as possible.'

'Do you still want me?' Mayor Digby asked.

'I've got to guard the money. You can stay and help if you want,' Marshal Douglas said.

'What?'

Dale answered Mayor Digby's question.

'As I've just agreed with Marshal Douglas, two of our wagon riders will take the wagon back to Beaver Ridge, straight away. Meanwhile, the rest of us are heading off to start the search for the bank raiders and Deputy Cassidy.'

Brett laughed silently.

'They really think you're a deputy,' he whispered.

'What? You're not guarding the money? What happens if those raiders come here?' Mayor Digby whined.

'I'm all the guarding you'll need,' Marshal Douglas said. 'With your help, of course.'

Brett beamed happily at Cassidy, and Cassidy remembered to smile back. He was losing track of when to look pleased and when to look forlorn. At every piece of good news for his plans he had to look unhappy, whereas this piece of disastrous news was the best result possible, if he'd been an outlaw.

'We'll just put the money in here when you're ready, then we'll be on our way,' Dale said.

Venturing to peer through the crack in the door, Cassidy could see Dale standing beside the bank door, his rifle resting on his thigh. Outside, two other wagon riders jumped into the wagon, and threw a collection of small bags to the ground. Cassidy wasn't a good judge of large sums of money, but he guessed that within the eight bags that he could see, there'd be enough for a small gang of outlaws. With the bags on the ground, one wagon rider strode to the bank, and spoke to Dale in the doorway.

Cassidy couldn't hear their conversation, but couldn't help but hear Mayor Digby whine.

'Marshal. You're not really expecting me to stay here for the next two days, while everyone arrives to collect their cash.'

'Why will it take two days?'

'Because the wagon is early, and no one bothered to tell me,' Mayor Digby snapped. 'Now, of course, if someone had bothered to keep me informed, I could have organized things differently, but oh no, I'm the last person to find out anything around here.'

'Enough!' Marshal Douglas shouted, then after a moment's pause, continued more softly, 'Let's just try to get along, or this is going to be a very long few days. I'll guard the money, just get someone trustworthy to help me.'

'What? Do you mean that you're going to create a new deputy? We didn't think much of the last deputy.'

Cassidy winced at this comment, and from the corner of his eye hazarded a glance at Brett to see how he reacted, but Brett still stood, waiting his moment to show his hand. Clearly, from Cassidy's actions over the last few days nobody would believe he was a deputy. Cassidy hoped that when his time came, he'd still be able to remember how to react properly.

'No new deputies,' Marshal Douglas shouted. 'I'll stay in the bank on my own. I just need someone to look in every so often.'

Mayor Digby mumbled to himself.

'Never had no trouble like this when Sheriff Wishbone was around.'

Brett tapped Cassidy on the arm, and whispered, 'This gets better and better.'

Cassidy nodded. Just as he began to ponder how he should react, now that the odds had changed significantly, a sudden thought came to mind. They knew the wagon riders were leaving straight away, but Daniel and Jason, outside, would not know this. To himself, he whispered, 'Daniel and Jason.'

'What you mean?' Brett whispered. As Cassidy turned to stare at him he could tell that Brett had the same thought. They stood staring at each other, sharing the mounting shock, though for different reasons.

'What we going to do?' Cassidy whispered, unsure as he said the words whether Daniel's explosive diversion would be a good thing or a bad thing.

Brett rubbed his damp forehead. 'Got to do something, or they'll ruin everything.'

Cassidy nodded, having decided that avoiding further explosions would be better than waiting for the more chaotic event afterwards.

He edged to the door to peer through the crack. Just inside the bank, he could see Marshal Douglas and Mayor Digby standing and staring in opposite directions in uncomfortable silence. The teller waited behind the counter staring at the both of them. In the doorway, Dale still stood guard, his rifle held loosely in his hand. Unable to see any more, Cassidy slowly opened the door a little further. In the wider gap he could see the open bank door. Outside, two wagon riders held the collection of bags in their arms, staring down the road at something or somebody.

Realizing that the time to stop Brett's sons acting was rapidly approaching, Cassidy swung to Brett and mouthed, 'Now.'

As Brett began to pull the door fully open, Cassidy stepped back a little, ready to pull his Peacemaker on Brett as soon as he emerged through the back office door.

Suddenly, the door exploded inward, and Cassidy realized that he was lying on his back on the floor. Glass tinkled around him, and a deep ringing resounded in his ears, filling his mind. Shaking his head, and confused, Cassidy pushed himself to his feet. He stumbled past Brett, who knelt on the ground holding his head, and staggered to the open door. Standing outside the back office, he stared at the inside of the bank, which was now a pitted, open wasteland. Paper fluttered around, and clouds of dust billowed across the room.

At Cassidy's feet Nathaniel knelt, also shaking his head. The teller lay beside him, his clothing shredded, his body slumped and still. After pushing the broken glass away from the counter with his arm, Cassidy staggered over the counter, and stood, trying to understand the scene before him. Tottering, he stared through the blackened, empty windows and doorway. Behind him, he heard Brett clambering over the counter too.

'What have they done?' Brett cried. He pushed past Cassidy, stumbling outside and into the road.

All thoughts of the bank raid drifted from Cassidy's mind as he stumbled to the door after him. At the door he coughed and spluttered for a few moments, clearing his lungs, and glanced back inside to see Marshal Douglas lying in a heap next to Mayor Digby. He tried to force himself to see if they were all right, but couldn't move back into the wrecked building. He felt desperate for pure air.

As if in a dream, he staggered outside, to be faced by a scene of carnage. As a child, he'd seen a number of sights resulting from the war that he didn't want to remember, but the blasted wreckage of the wagon was as bad as he'd seen for a while. The wagon riders all lay sprawled about the wagon in postures they'd never naturally assume, and if any were still alive, Cassidy prayed they wouldn't last long.

Some yards into the road, he saw Brett stagger between each mangled corpse, kicking at each as he went. Cassidy wondered for a moment what he was doing, then remembered that his sons had created this explosion. He doubted Brett would find what he looked for amongst this unplanned level of devastation.

Feeling a little ashamed, Cassidy slithered his Peacemaker from his holster, and waited until he saw Brett fall to his knees beside two foreshortened heaps. Despite all the death that Brett had helped to cause, he resolved to give Brett a few moments, before arresting him.

Surprising him, Nathaniel patted a hand on Cassidy's shoulder, and whispered:

'Looks like you were right, dynamite doesn't always do as it's told.'

Cassidy nodded, although he felt no pleasure that events had proved him right.

'Nathaniel, Cassidy, get the bags. We're out of here!' Brett suddenly shouted.

Shaking his head to free the ringing that still bounced back and forth in his head, Cassidy wandered forward a few paces, pushed the body of a wagon rider aside, and grabbed one bag. Then he realized what he was doing. Slowly he stood straight, and stared at Brett. The time for being an outlaw had finally ended.

Ten yards in front of him, facing the bank, Brett kicked at the body of another wagon rider, pushed him away from two of the bags, and hefted them.

'Come on, Nathaniel, Cassidy, we've got a long way to go.'

'You're not leaving Jason and Daniel, are you?' Nathaniel shouted.

'Sure am, too late for them, idiots that they were.'

Cassidy couldn't postpone any longer. He waited until both Nathaniel and Brett had backed a few paces, then aimed his Peacemaker at them.

'Sorry, no one is going anywhere.'

'What do you mean?' Brett asked as he spun towards him, and glanced down at Cassidy's gun. 'Put it away, Cassidy, we'll split three ways, and that'll be enough for us all.'

'Sure won't. I'm not letting you walk from here.'

Brett grinned, and throwing his hands from his body, dropped the bags to the ground.

'You'll never shoot us both before we stop you. No matter who you take, you'll not be the one walking from here.'

'Correction,' another voice from behind Cassidy said. 'I'm not letting anyone walk away from here. All of you put you hands on your heads, real slow.'

Cassidy recognized the voice as belonging to Marshal Douglas, and relaxed, feeling his life slip back into the familiar pattern of a lawman. Slowly, he holstered his gun, and placed his hands on his head. Having Marshal Douglas arrest him caused him no worry; he trusted the man.

Brett spat on the ground.

'Must be getting old, and careless, I assumed you'd be blown to pieces like these here wagon riders.'

Marshal Douglas shook his head, and patted a little dust from his clothes.

'Takes more than a little explosion to kill me. Don't matter none now, I'm taking all three of you in. Just throw your guns down, reach, and we'll all go for a little walk to the cells.'

Brett stood his ground.

'Three against one, Marshal, don't sound like good odds to me.'

Feeling himself relax as his true role as lawman began to emerge, Cassidy smiled.

'You're wrong, Brett, it's two against two.'

After a quick glance at Cassidy, Brett laughed, and muttered:

'Stop it, Cassidy. Whatever your problem with me is, we can sort it out together, later, but don't side with the marshal, you'll never profit from it.'

Cassidy didn't care about any profit, but he knew that the second he admitted to being a lawman, Brett would go for his Adams. From his having shot Sheriff Wishbone, Cassidy guessed that he was fast. His own death didn't worry Cassidy; what concerned him more was that when Marshal Douglas reacted, Nathaniel was going to die too. Nathaniel was the only one of Brett's family who appeared to have the slightest bit of decency; he'd not killed anybody during their outlawing, and Cassidy was sure that with better influences he'd turn out to be a fine man. If he could defuse the situation, Nathaniel might even get that chance. Just as important, Cassidy owed him a debt, and he hated the thought of not repaying.

Slowly, Cassidy turned to Marshal Douglas.

'Marshal, you got no reason to trust me, but let me talk to Brett.'

From over his shoulder, Brett shouted:

'No time for talking, we're going.'

'You're going nowhere,' Marshal Douglas pronounced. 'One more pace, in any direction, from any of you, and you're all dead men.'

'Brett,' Cassidy shouted, 'Marshal Douglas is the fastest lawman on the draw I've ever heard about. You've just lost two sons, and you're about to lose the last.'

After wiggling his fingers, shuffling his feet, and hunching slightly, Brett whispered, 'Won't lose nobody. I know I'm faster.'

Glancing at Marshal Douglas, Cassidy saw the lawman step back to get a clear shot at all three of them. Realizing that this matter was about to be cleared very quickly, Cassidy shouted, 'You will lose Nathaniel, because I intend to kill him.'

Brett slowly turned to stare at Cassidy as he lifted his hands from his head, and hunched forward towards Nathaniel.

'You wouldn't,' Brett said.

Cassidy stared at Nathaniel, who did his best to appear committed and tough. Unfortunately, from his slightly hen-toed stance, Cassidy guessed that Nathaniel had never tried to pull his gun in anger in a fast draw, at least in the company of other men.

Cassidy nodded his head sadly.

'I would,' he said.

'I'll kill you, if you do,' Brett shouted.

'You might at that.'

Cassidy stared at Marshal Douglas as the lawman steadily edged around in a circle. Cassidy could tell from his new position he could spray his shots across Brett and Nathaniel, so he wasn't going to take Cassidy out too.

'If you shoot me, Marshal Douglas will get you, then take out Nathaniel. If you go for Marshal Douglas, I'll kill your last son, then take you out, if you win.'

With his eyes narrowed, Brett whispered, 'I'm too fast, you'll never get me.'

From the confidence in Brett's voice, Cassidy guessed that he might be right.

'Probably, but either way, Nathaniel still dies.'

'You heard Cassidy. Give up, Brett,' Marshal Douglas said.

Nathaniel flexed his arms vigorously.

'Don't listen to him, Pa, I can take care of myself,' he shouted.

Cassidy laughed.

'Yeah, just like your idiot brothers, Jason and Daniel.'

'Why you . . . ' Brett screamed, and flourished his hand.

Immediately, Cassidy thrust his own hand down, grabbed his Peacemaker, and in an instant fired at Nathaniel, blasting the gun from his hand while it was still half-way out of its holster.

As two other gunshots echoed around him, Cassidy glanced quickly from Brett to Marshal Douglas, who both stood, guns drawn, small swirls of smoke drifting across the road between them. Cassidy hunched forward, ready to take Brett. Then he noticed the plume of dirt fading to nothing a few feet in front of Brett, who slowly fell backward, to land with a grunt on the ground.

Clutching his gun hand in his other hand, Nathaniel dashed to his father, but Cassidy could see the rose of blood spreading across Brett's chest, and knew that his moments were numbered.

He glanced at Marshal Douglas who, with a swift spin of his hand, thrust his own .45 back in his holster. Then he nodded to Cassidy.

'Right you two, off to the cells,' he said.

'There's no need to lock me up, Marshal.'

'Am I right in thinking from that request that you're Deputy Cassidy Yates?'

'Sure am, although I prefer Deputy Cassidy. You don't need to put me in a cell, I'm on your side of the law.' With these words, Cassidy relaxed. He'd wanted to say this to someone who would believe him for the last few days.

Marshal Douglas shook his head, then waved his hand towards Sheriff Wishbone's old office.

'I'm sure you are, and I expect you're not guilty of Sheriff Wishbone's murder, or any of the things Mayor Digby seems to think you're responsible for.'

'Mayor Digby,' Cassidy snapped. 'No, I'm not guilty of anything that man thinks I've done.'

'That's as maybe, but you're guilty of everything else.'

'What else? I only stayed with Brett's gang to make sure they failed, and that no one else was hurt.' Cassidy tailed off; his excuse sounded too pathetic as he uttered it, surrounded as he was with the sprawled bodies of over a dozen lawmen.

Marshal Douglas waved behind him at the wagon, and the bodies sprawled around him.

'You forgot you were a lawman, and this is the result.'

Although he didn't feel completely responsible for everything that had happened, Cassidy hung his head in shame. He stepped over to Brett's body. Noting that Brett was now dead, he reached down and clutched Nathaniel around the shoulders. Nathaniel didn't shrug away as he'd expected, but stared up with watering eyes.

'Got no family now,' he mumbled.

'Come on, let's move on,' Cassidy said, finding nothing to say that wouldn't appear trite in the circumstances. Without complaint, he led Nathaniel to Sheriff Wishbone's office.

Standing outside the cell inside which Sheriff Wishbone had locked him only a few days ago, Cassidy turned to Marshal Douglas.

'I tried to lessen the damage. I did my best,' he said.

Marshal Douglas said nothing until Cassidy was inside the cell.

'Your best wasn't good enough. Once you're a lawman, you're always a lawman. You don't pretend to be an outlaw, and hope to make things better. You betrayed the badge, and yourself.'

Feeling this criticism was unfair, Cassidy gripped the bars.

'You're wrong. I felt trapped on all sides. What could I do?'

At the door, Marshal Douglas stood, turned away, and shook his head.

'Die, that's what you could have done, but at least you'd have died a lawman. A lawman never abandons his duty, and you did.'

Once Marshal Douglas had slammed the door, Cassidy glanced into the corner of his cell, where Nathaniel sat on his bunk, and stared at the wall. Cassidy didn't hold much hope of making a connection there either, but deciding to try anyway, he mumbled:

'Nathaniel, I'll make sure you don't take the blame here. What you did will only get you a few years in jail.'

'Don't speak to me,' Nathaniel mumbled, and drew his legs up to his chin.

Feeling totally dismissed by everyone whom he'd tried to help, Cassidy settled on his bunk, and began to prepare for the final erosion of his life as a lawman.

13

While Nathaniel sat on his wrecked bunk, Cassidy slouched against the wall. With the silence dragging on him, he shuffled round, and stared through the cell window. Holding on to the cool bars, he rested his chin on the sill, and stared across the road.

A few of the inhabitants of Redemption City had now strayed closer to the carnage beside the bank. Cassidy could see that Marshal Douglas had organized a few of them to form an informal barrier to stop too many people coming close. The carnage was a sight that would do nobody any good to see.

Moving quickly from body to body, a man who was presumably a doctor knelt beside each body. Cassidy was pleased to note that the doctor ordered a small group of people, who followed him around, to carry three of the bodies away into a nearby building. Presumably these victims weren't dead, and perhaps even had a hope of recovery, or he doubted that the doctor would bother to try to help.

Suddenly Cassidy noticed Mayor Digby wandering from the wrecked bank, covered in dust but apparently unharmed. Allowing a little grunt of irritation to escape his lips, Cassidy watched the mayor stand framed in the blasted bank doorway. Silently, Mayor Digby stared at Marshal Douglas's back as he dragged a body towards a cart that someone had brought close to the twisted wreckage of the wagon.

Cassidy watched the mayor do nothing to help in the thankless task, and as he stared, Cassidy wondered what disagreement the mayor and Marshal Douglas might have had. From the conversation he'd overheard in the bank, the two of them had argued before, but he couldn't decide over what.

For the next ten minutes he watched

Marshal Douglas personally lift each body on to the cart. Cassidy could see that the marshal was the sort of person who kept to his creed, and never abandoned his duty, even for terrible tasks like this. Cassidy counted twelve bodies in all, including Brett McBain's, after which the marshal piled the bags of money that the wagon had delivered outside the bank. He ordered some people to guard the bags. Cassidy shook his head; even after all the wagon riders had died or been badly injured, Marshal Douglas still ensured that he completed his duty.

'It's true, a lawman never abandons his duty,' Cassidy whispered to himself. Although, he suddenly realized, the wagon riders were about to leave town, abandoning their duty, apparently something they did every month, according to Brett's previous observation.

Cassidy stared at Marshal Douglas standing over the bags of money, and Mayor Digby still standing in the bank doorway and, with a sudden quickening of his heart-beat, he realized that something was wrong here. Something had always been wrong. Decent, law-abiding, God-fearing people shouldn't try to lynch the first man they find for a killing. Town mayors don't fall out with marshals, and whine about cash deliveries at banks, and, most important, a lawman never abandons his duty. Marshal Douglas doesn't, but the wagon riders did.

After pushing himself from the window, Cassidy hung his head for a moment, unable to decide if the wild ideas surging through his mind were plausible. Undecided, he stared around the cell, and realized that no matter how much trouble he was in, acting now couldn't increase his problems, but might stop something worse happening.

He patted his pockets; flat inside his jacket was the slip of metal that he'd used to break into the bank. This discovery made Cassidy's mind up for him; he strode to the cell door, slipped his hand through the bars, and after a few moments of fiddling, managed to lever the lock.

Standing in the doorway to the main office, he glanced back at Nathaniel, who sat, knees drawn up to his chin, lost in his own private hell. Cassidy ignored him, stormed into the office and, after rummaging in the office desk and pulling out his Peacemaker, dashed to the door.

Outside, he strode confidently across the road towards Marshal Douglas, all the time keeping one eye on Mayor Digby.

'Marshal,' Mayor Digby shouted, and pointed at Cassidy. 'Look, one of your charges is trying to escape.'

To avoid raising concern, Cassidy lifted his gun hand above his head, but still kept two fingers looped so he could quickly react if Mayor Digby did anything.

Marshal Douglas shook his head.

'Cassidy, you ain't making this easy for yourself, get back in the cell.'

Cassidy kept striding towards Marshal Douglas, only stopping when ten paces away from him.

'Marshal, we need to talk.'

'There's nothing you can say to me now. I've a task to do, and all you can do is let me finish it,' Marshal Douglas said. Slowly, he glanced around, with his arms outstretched, indicating the wrecked wagon, the dead wagon riders and bags of money as comprising the task that he still had to complete. 'You had your chance, and you ruined it. There's nothing you can do that'll improve matters, but you need to ensure you don't make things worse. All you can contribute now is to wait for me in your cell, and let me take you back to Beaver Ridge, without complaint.'

'Marshal, just answer me one question.' Marshal Douglas didn't say anything, but only scowled at Cassidy a little deeper. Taking this as his permission to continue talking, Cassidy pressed on. 'You said that a lawman never abandons his duty, and you're right, so why did the wagon riders leave the cash here, unprotected, except for you, before the companies out west arrived to collect it?'

With this question, Mayor Digby finally strode from his position beside the bank, and marched forward to stand alongside Marshal Douglas.

'Why have you let this outlaw out of his cell, Marshal?'

'He's going back in his cell, head first, in a few seconds, just as soon as I've answered his pathetic question,' Marshal Douglas muttered to Mayor Digby, and then swirled round to stare at Cassidy. 'The wagon riders were going in search of Sheriff Wishbone's killer; they weren't to know he was already here, waiting, with the sheriff's deputy.'

With this pronouncement, Marshal Douglas strode towards Cassidy, who backed a pace and nodded towards the moneybags lying midway between Mayor Digby and Marshal Douglas.

'Don't forget the money bags, Marshal. I wouldn't leave them out here. You don't know what types might seize the opportunity for a little stealing.'

Marshal Douglas stopped, spun round, and stared at the moneybags, then darted a glance back and forward between the cash and Cassidy.

'All right, I suppose I can trust you to help with just this one task. You take four bags, I'll take the other four.'

Mayor Digby strode between them, and stared at Marshal Douglas.

'You ain't going to let him touch the money, are you?'

'Sure am, he's still a lawman, despite his mistakes.'

All of Mayor Digby's nervous reactions only encouraged Cassidy to know that he was right. By all rights, he should wait until they were back in the sheriff's office before voicing his theories, but Mayor Digby had annoyed him too much over the last few days. Without thinking, Cassidy asked the question he'd thought of in the cell.

'You're telling me, Marshal, that the only reason the wagon riders left the money unguarded in Redemption City was because Sheriff Wishbone is now dead, and they were after his killer.'

'Yup, now grab these bags.'

Feeling annoyance bubble over, Cassidy grabbed Mayor Digby by the shoulder, swinging him round to stare into his face.

'Is that true, Mayor Digby? Do the wagon riders always stay until all the cash is in the right hands? Is this the only delivery that they haven't stayed behind to guard, until they have discharged their duty?'

Mayor Digby shook in his grasp, failing to push away Cassidy's strong grip on his shoulders.

'I wouldn't know. I don't concern myself in such matters.'

Poised, kneeling on the ground as he gathered a collection of bags together, Marshal Douglas stared up at Cassidy.

'What you getting at, Cassidy?'

Before he answered, Cassidy glanced

down the road. With the bodies removed, a number of other people had strayed into the middle of the road. He could see Bill McGruder and Jake Grounding, plus a few others he recognized from when the town had tried to lynch him, and steadily they were edging closer.

Backing slightly from Mayor Digby, Cassidy whispered, 'Marshal, something is wrong here, very wrong.'

Marshal Douglas glanced over his shoulder at the approaching townsfolk, and whilst staring at them, laughed, and said, 'Don't worry, Cassidy. I'll make sure you get a fair trial in Beaver Ridge. These folk won't try to lynch you.'

'What, again?' Cassidy spat.

'Again?' Marshal Douglas said, wheeling round to stare at Cassidy. 'What do you mean by again?'

'Watch out,' Mayor Digby shouted.

Cassidy spun round, staring up and down the road, torn between multiple possibilities for what to look out for; then he saw Marshal Douglas, staring past his shoulder, slowly straighten up. Cassidy turned right round; behind him was Nathaniel, standing beside the cart which now contained his father's body, and in his hand was his father's Adams.

'Put down that gun, now,' Marshal Douglas shouted. 'If you don't, I'll be forced to kill you.'

Cassidy lifted one arm, and shouted, 'Wait, let me talk to him.'

Ignoring Mayor Digby, who muttered something under his breath, Cassidy strode a pace towards Nathaniel, before Nathaniel turned his Adams towards him.

'No further, Cassidy, you'll be the first to get it,' Nathaniel shouted.

'Don't do it, Nathaniel.'

'Why? Got nothing left any more.'

Cassidy shook his head, hating to hear such a young man say something so negative. He held his arms wide, far from his Peacemaker.

'You've got everything. A new life, and a far better life than if you shoot me.'

'All that matters is making sure you don't live, after what you did to my pa.'

Staring down the barrel of Nathaniel's Adams, Cassidy knew the time for avoiding the issue had passed.

'Sorry, Nathaniel, but I'm not responsible for what happened to your pa.'

Nathaniel glanced at Marshal Douglas, then back at Cassidy, his eyes wild.

'I saw what happened. You and Marshal Douglas together did it. I don't know which one pulled the trigger, but Marshal Douglas was only doing his duty. You're worse. I saved your life; you pretended to be part of our gang, our family, then you turned on us, just like you always intended to do.'

Cassidy knew that betraying someone's trust was almost as bad as anything that Brett had done. In this case, he had had no choice, not that he'd find it easy to explain this to a man ready to avenge his father's death. Searching for a compromise, he said:

'When I said I wasn't responsible, I meant that your pa chose his path, and he chose the wrong one, for all his family, and for you too.'

'My pa did what he thought was best, you can't judge him,' Nathaniel shouted, lifting his Adams a little higher.

From the corner of his eye, Cassidy saw Marshal Douglas turn, gaining a clear view of Nathaniel. Cassidy realized that his argument was on the wrong track, and only a different approach would defuse the situation.

'Your pa was a lethal gunfighter, there's no way Marshal Douglas could defeat him. Brett knew I wouldn't kill you, and lost deliberately, so that you could have a better life than living as a wanted outlaw.'

Cassidy glanced at Marshal Douglas, who gave a small nod back. Cassidy didn't know whether he was right about what had happened or not, but there had to be a possibility that Brett had deliberately lost. Truth or not, this version of events was the only one that was likely to save Nathaniel.

Gulping, and running an arm over his forehead, Nathaniel shouted, 'He didn't, he was outnumbered.'

'Two against two ain't outnumbered.'

'You saying I'm like Jason and Daniel, all stupid, unable to count?'

Cassidy winced; he hadn't meant his comment like that. He advanced a small space, and tried to explain himself a little better. 'Your pa wasn't scared of anybody, because he could out-think, or outshoot himself from any situation. He'd have killed Marshal Douglas and me easily, but I don't think he wanted the two of you to be running and hiding for the rest of your lives. He wanted you to have a proper chance.'

From behind him, Marshal Douglas said, 'Cassidy, step aside, I'll deal with this.'

Cassidy shook his head, determined to prove he could still deal with problems in the right way.

'No, I'll talk him back to the cell. I

know he's a good lad. He saved my life. He's decent.'

From behind him, Mayor Digby grunted.

'Don't trust him, they're working together.'

Cassidy spun round, to see Mayor Digby had hefted two bags.

'What you doing?'

While shuffling the two bags further into his arms, Mayor Digby muttered, 'I'm moving the cash out of your way, before you get your thieving hands on it.'

Realizing that Mayor Digby had already gone too far, Cassidy abandoned his talk with Nathaniel, slowly drew his Peacemaker, and pointed it at Mayor Digby.

'Put those bags down, or you're dead.'

'I don't know what you think you're doing, but stop this. Press on any further, and I won't be able to help you,' Marshal Douglas shouted. He turned away from Nathaniel, drawing his .45 on Cassidy.

Cassidy shook his head.

'I don't know exactly what's going on in Redemption City, but I reckon Brett was right. Any chain is as strong as its weakest link. As far as I can make out, that weak link is in Redemption City, and I'm looking at the weakest link of them all, right now. Put the bags down, Mayor Digby, and step away.'

Mayor Digby glanced over Cassidy's shoulder, and then at Marshal Douglas.

'We're surrounded. He's got Nathaniel with a gun on you, and his gun is on me. Marshal, stop them.'

Marshal Douglas appeared to ignore Mayor Digby's plea, but he narrowed his eyes, and glared directly at Cassidy.

'What's your point, Cassidy?'

Realizing that the time for discussion had passed, that now he had to state his fears openly, Cassidy stared at Mayor Digby's small form. He spoke deliberately slowly.

'I've no idea what scam is going on here, but the wagon riders left the money to search for Brett McBain this month. This is something they should only do in exceptional circumstances, but they do it every month. That's why Brett decided to raid here.'

As he heard these words Mayor Digby threw down the bags and, with a little squeal, dived to the ground.

Working on pure, instinctive self-preservation Cassidy dived to the ground too, just as gunfire ricocheted all around him. He scrambled over the ground to land beside the body-cart, closely followed by Marshal Douglas. Twenty paces in front of them, a row of townsfolk dashed for cover behind the wrecked wagon, firing wildly as they ran.

Deciding that protecting the innocents was impossible when the whole town was guilty, Cassidy fired off three shots in a continuous burst of gunfire, catching two men before they reached cover.

During a small lull, they swung behind the body-cart, to find Nathaniel, hunched down. Without time to check on where Nathaniel's loyalties lay, Cassidy grabbed the underside of the cart, and tugged upward, but the bodies sprawled inside made the weight too much. Seeing what he was doing, Marshal Douglas grabbed the cart too, and so did Nathaniel. At first the body-cart didn't move, then, two bodies slipped from the back of the cart, and with a sickening series of thuds the cart toppled over.

Only then, with a complete screened protection, did they duck behind the cart. Cassidy turned to Marshal Douglas.

'What are we going to do now?'

Marshal Douglas grinned, and flexed his fingers.

'Fight.'

Cassidy nodded; this went without saying, and curiously, although massively out-numbered, and with little hope of survival, he felt happier than at any time since he'd first arrived in Redemption City.

Now he could be a lawman and, if necessary, die as a lawman.

14

Kneeling down while he reloaded, Cassidy glanced at Nathaniel.

'You've got a choice, Nathaniel. Join us, or go against us. What's it to be?'

Nathaniel glanced at Marshal Douglas, then back at Cassidy, and slowly nodded.

'The way I see it, either way I'm not walking out of here alive.'

Marshal Douglas clamped a hand on his shoulder. 'Better to die a lawman than as an outlaw.'

'I'm no lawman,' Nathaniel snapped, shrugging his hand away.

'You are, if I say you are.'

Slowly, Nathaniel smiled. 'Pa wouldn't like that.'

Cassidy shook his head. 'Your pa would like that, he wanted the best for you.'

'Even if the best is dying.'

'Depends what you're dying for,' Marshal Douglas said.

Nathaniel glanced at Cassidy. 'Is that true?'

Cassidy had never been surer of anything in his life. 'Sure is.'

Marshal Douglas patted both Cassidy and Nathaniel on the shoulder, before glancing over the top of the cart, and ducking down again. He waited until a cascade of gunfire exploded over the top of the cart, then stared at them.

'There's ten, maybe twelve of them, lying down, fanned out across the road. I'm guessing they aren't good shots or they'd have got us already.'

'What's your instructions?' Cassidy asked.

'Keep it simple, and move fast, and we might just get through this.' Marshal Douglas pointed at him. 'Cassidy, on five, you come out of the left side.'

Cassidy nodded, pleased to be taking commands again.

Marshal Douglas turned to Nathaniel,

and held a hand on his shoulder.

'Nathaniel, also on five, you come out on the right.'

Nathaniel stared at the ground, shaking his head.

'I wasn't going to shoot you back there. I know what my pa did was wrong.'

Suddenly, Marshal Douglas clamped a hand over Nathaniel's mouth.

'Enough, you can't worry about that now, it's not important, just concentrate on surviving the next few minutes.'

Slowly, he lifted his hand, and Nathaniel nodded, and mumbled, 'All right.'

At this Marshal Douglas quickly checked his .45.

'While you two go out on your sides, I'll go over the top of the cart,' he said. 'We shoot at anybody close, and head for the bank.'

Cassidy nodded, and shuffled along the ground to the side of the cart. When they were both ready, he watched

Marshal Douglas count down on his fingers. On five he threw himself from behind the cart. He hit the ground, rolled on to his stomach, and fired three times at the nearest man, who twitched, then collapsed face down in the dirt.

Cassidy leapt to his feet and ran, crouching, for the bank, shooting his gun until it was empty at the nearest gun-toters, getting one more before his scrabbling run reached the bank. Once there, he glanced around, to see that Nathaniel had leapt through the empty window-frame, and now stood, reloading. But Marshal Douglas wasn't in the bank. Hazarding a quick glance outside, Cassidy saw that the Marshal had gained cover behind the wrecked wagon, in front of the bank. He could also see four bodies sprawled on their backs on the ground, so the odds had been considerably lessened. Now they just needed some luck.

'Marshal,' Mayor Digby shouted, 'we can sort this out.'

Cassidy looked beyond the bodies to

see Mayor Digby standing, arms raised, in the plumb centre of the road. In annoyance, Cassidy slammed his hand against the wall. If he'd seen Mayor Digby on his dash for the bank, he'd have made sure he got a bullet, even if he was unarmed.

'I can hardly arrest a whole town, Mayor Digby,' Marshal Douglas shouted, 'but if your men here throw in their guns, then we'll talk.'

Cassidy coughed, clearing his throat.

'Don't trust him, Marshal, this whole town has a secret to protect, they won't let us leave.'

Cassidy slipped into the bank doorway, and stared at the road to see that their assailants were leaping to their feet and quickly grouping together behind Mayor Digby. Cassidy recognized Bill McGruder, George Rogers and Jake Grounding and some others who had sat in judgement over his lynching. He counted nine of them. Whatever corruption existed in this town, Cassidy guessed it was limited to these men.

Mayor Digby strode confidently towards Marshal Douglas.

'Marshal, I'm unarmed, let's talk this through. There has clearly been a deep misunderstanding.'

'Don't trust him,' Cassidy shouted; he'd had enough of misunderstandings in Redemption City.

Marshal Douglas lifted one hand and strode from behind the wagon.

'What do you propose, Mayor Digby?'

Ten yards back from the wagon, Mayor Digby stopped.

'I don't want to talk to an armed man, not one who has shot four of my townsfolk. Let us talk, unarmed man to unarmed man.'

After a few moments' silence, Marshal Douglas nodded.

'All right, but back here, behind the wagon, out of the line of fire of your men.'

'Don't do this, Marshal, that man tried to lynch me!' Cassidy shouted.

Marshal Douglas lifted an arm.

'Cassidy, this is my decision to make. The sooner you start following orders, the sooner you'll remember how to be a proper lawman again, and stop making stupid mistakes like joining up with Brett McBain.'

Hanging his head slightly, Cassidy realized this criticism was totally justified. Quietly now, he watched Mayor Digby nod and stride around the side of the wagon, towards Marshal Douglas. Cassidy did his best to watch Mayor Digby, and his men behind the wagon, who all shuffled as if they were getting ready for action. He would have shouted a warning, but didn't want to distract, or annoy, Marshal Douglas any further.

Once Mayor Digby stood in front of Marshal Douglas, the lawman carefully placed his .45 close to him on top of the wagon in case he needed it again, then turned to Mayor Digby.

'So, how do we sort this out?'

'Like this; let me show you some evidence that might convince you that things aren't quite what they seem.' Moving his hand slowly, Mayor Digby slipped his hand into his jacket, and then, in a sudden movement, yanked a pistol out, firing instantly.

As Marshal Douglas crumbled to the ground, the men behind the wagon sprayed the bank with a continuous round of gunfire.

Without time to do anything constructive, Cassidy threw himself to ground as the gunfire ripped across the doorway. Kneeling on the ground beside the door, Cassidy could hear the men outside dashing across the road towards the bank. Feverishly, Cassidy glanced around the wrecked room, to see that after the explosion there was little cover available.

Cassidy glanced at Nathaniel, who stared back and shouted:

'What're we going to do?'

For a few seconds Cassidy bit his bottom lip while he tried to think of some plan. The gun-toters outside surrounded and outnumbered them; in a few seconds this was all going to be over.

'Don't rightly know.'

'You'd better think of something. I've got no idea, and we ain't got long.'

Suddenly, brightening, Cassidy asked, 'What would your pa have done in this situation?'

Nathaniel smiled. 'He'd sooner try and fail, than do nothing; he'd have done the unexpected, and stormed out of here firing at anything that moved. He wouldn't have stayed and waited for them to pick us off.'

This suggestion was closer to a plan than any other choices available. Cassidy accepted they needed to act before the men outside gained impregnable positions to take them at their leisure. Although they had little chance of success, Cassidy nodded.

'All right, on three,' he said. 'You take the left, I'll take the right.'

So, on the count of three he dived through the door, rolled to his feet, and sprayed a line of continuous fire across the three nearest men. Behind him, he could hear Nathaniel clatter from the window, and shoot at the men approaching from the left.

Without time to see where his shots landed, Cassidy leapt for the wagon. He could see Mayor Digby cowering on the ground next to Marshal Douglas's body, and with his gun dry, Cassidy kicked him full in the face, then leapt for Marshall Douglas's .45, lying on the wagon.

He grabbed the gun and threw himself over the wagon, bullets ripping into the side as he fell. He landed awkwardly, with the wagon at his back. He tried to stagger to his feet, the .45 still pointed down as he stumbled, then, looking up, he saw that he faced a line of four men in front of him.

As he righted his stance he saw George Rogers on the far left of the line of men, and on the far right stood Bill McGruder, who nodded at him.

'Some fancy shooting there,' he said.

'So, do you two want to give yourselves up, or shall we kill you here?'

Realizing that Nathaniel was still alive, Cassidy glanced to his left to see Nathaniel kneeling on the ground beside the wagon. At his feet was his Adams, one hand was poised with a handful of bullets, ready to reload. Neither he nor Cassidy would get a chance to fire before the four men cut them down.

Cassidy flexed his fingers, deciding that he'd at least get Bill McGruder, the card-cheat, even if the rest cut him to shreds. From his left, he heard Mayor Digby shout:

'Go on, what you waiting for? Shoot them.'

'Can't shoot unarmed men, Mayor,' Bill McGruder answered, in an unexpected hint of normality in this mad situation.

'They are armed, you idiots.' With this, Mayor Digby kicked Nathaniel's Adams away, and with the back of his hand slapped Nathaniel across the face.

With the young man prone before him, Mayor Digby kicked him squarely on the chin, making him rise up to land hard on his back.

Glancing at the four men he faced, Cassidy saw that all of them were momentarily distracted by this fight. Deciding this was the only chance he'd get, Cassidy fired at Bill, and threw himself to his left. He felt gunfire explode around his feet. Running as fast as he could, he made for Nathaniel and Mayor Digby. He barged into them, knocking Mayor Digby to the ground, then he dragged him to his feet and stood behind him. After spinning Mayor Digby round, he faced the three men in front.

Gaining his breath with a couple of quick gulps, Cassidy shouted:

'Right, now you three put your guns down, reach, and we'll head for the cells.'

'Three against one aren't good odds,' George Rogers shouted.

Cassidy wrapped his arm further

around Mayor Digby's neck; he felt the Mayor gasp and struggle ineffectually with his arms waving wildly.

'That'll be four against one,' Bill McGruder said, staggering to his feet and holding his arm.

Lifting his .45 closer to Mayor Digby's head, Cassidy lowered his voice.

'Put your guns down,' he said slowly, 'or Mayor Digby gets it.'

Bill laughed. 'You won't do anything, lawmen don't take hostages, or kill them.'

'I wouldn't bet on it,' Cassidy snarled, pressing his .45 to Mayor Digby's head.

Normally, Bill would have been right; as a lawman Cassidy would never take a hostage or would definitely never kill a hostage, but Mayor Digby had pushed him too far. This time he would have no compunction in avoiding his duty to protect innocent bystanders. Mayor Digby was as far from innocent as any man could go.

'Looks like a stand-off, Cassidy,' Bill shouted.

Although he had no qualms in killing Mayor Digby, his problem was what would happen then. He couldn't take all four of these men. Quickly, he glanced at Nathaniel, who still appeared out cold, and even if he came to his senses soon, he was around ten yards from his gun.

With little choice, Cassidy shouted, 'What do you propose?'

As Bill scratched his head, Mayor Digby whispered:

'You'll get nothing, Cassidy, whatever happens here, you don't get to walk away.'

Mayor Digby was right, and feeling that he needed one question answered before the end, Cassidy asked:

'Tell me, I don't care what was going on here, but did Sheriff Wishbone know what you were doing?'

'No,' Mayor Digby said. 'He was a good lawman, but not very intelligent.'

Cassidy doubted Sheriff Wishbone

was unintelligent, but even if he was, knowing that the lawman here hadn't been corrupt cheered him; at least something in this mad town made sense. He decided to accept this as the truth.

'Right,' he shouted, 'we are backing away, and you'll do the same, one steady pace at a time, or I'll shoot your Mayor.'

He must have sounded determined because Cassidy could feel Mayor Digby trembling in his grip. Leaning away from him, Mayor Digby shouted:

'You heard, don't take chances, he'll kill me. Back off.'

'Coward,' Bill shouted, and fired his gun. Mayor Digby staggered back against Cassidy.

Not pausing any more, Cassidy swung his .45 in an arc across the men starting with Bill McGruder and ending at George Rogers, pulsing his hand and finger rapidly as the gunfire filled his mind. More bullets pummelled into Mayor Digby's lifeless body as Cassidy staggered back and fell to the ground. Quickly, he dragged himself from under Mayor Digby's body, but all the men were down.

Not taking any chances, Cassidy reloaded Marshal Douglas's .45, then stood for long minutes waiting to see if anyone else attacked. But the few people who strayed from the shops and saloon didn't come close enough to threaten him. Cassidy had no idea how far or how deep the corruption in this town spread, but he didn't care; the only important thing was to get back to the normal world as quick as possible, and get proper help. Edging sideways, he moved towards Nathaniel, who was already stirring and shaking himself.

'Nathaniel, get ready to get out of here.'

Nathaniel glanced at the bodies sprawled around him, and gratifyingly didn't waste time asking questions. While he waited for Nathaniel to regain his senses, Cassidy checked Marshal Douglas, but the lawman lay with his mouth wide open; at short range the pistol had blasted a wide hole in his chest.

Cassidy hated leaving bodies unburied. He also knew that someone else in Redemption City might emerge to attack them. Wasting no time, he turned away from Marshal Douglas's body, strode down the road, and grabbed the reins of the two nearest horses from outside the saloon. Back at the bank, he quickly loaded them with the moneybags.

As he lifted himself on to his horse, Nathaniel asked, 'How much you reckon is in them, Cassidy?'

Cassidy glared at him a second, wondering if Nathaniel had misinterpreted the battle that had just taken place, then saw that the young man had no hint of avarice in the way he stared at the bags. Cassidy shook his head.

'Whatever is in there, is hardly worth the number of men who died trying to take it,' he observed.

They turned from the wrecked bank, the ruined wagon and the sprawl of bodies, and trotted away from Redemption City. Although there had to be a chance someone would follow, Cassidy didn't hurry or look back; Redemption City was one place he wouldn't run from, or to which he'd ever return. He kept a steady canter through Redemption City, avoiding meeting the eyes of the few people who lined the road and stared at them. He concentrated on keeping his back straight, his stare directly ahead, and his mind as far from the corrupted taint of Redemption City as possible.

As they passed the last store, Nathaniel turned to him.

'Where are we going?'

'Beaver Ridge, to finally sort this mess out.'

Speaking softly, Nathaniel said, 'How do you know I won't attack you, steal the money, and run?'

Judging his question to be neither light-hearted nor of serious intent,

Cassidy decided to provide an honest answer.

'I reckon you've run for too long already. Time now to face up to a new life.'

Nathaniel steered his horse closer.

'How long do you reckon I'll get in jail?'

Cassidy liked this question far more than he had the other questions, and it finally ended his fears for this young man's future.

'Depends.'

'On what?'

Cassidy turned to Nathaniel and offered him the truth of the life he had chosen to take many years ago; one he'd almost lost sight of over the last few days.

'Remember what Marshal Douglas said. All lawmen finish what they have started, and they never abandon their duty.'

They rode quietly for a few moments, the few shacks dotted around outside Redemption City giving way to open scrub-land. If Brett had given his son a chance of a new life, then Cassidy would ensure he got it; even if Brett hadn't, he still could.

Nathaniel turned to Cassidy.

'You once said that you were in my debt. Are you repaying that debt now by suggesting I'd make a lawman?' he asked.

Cassidy considered this question; he hadn't forgotten that promise, but trying to encourage Nathaniel to become a lawman didn't feel the appropriate way to repay him, not after all the death back in Redemption City.

'No, I'm still in your debt. I just think you'll make a fine lawman, and if you finish this job satisfactorily, no one need ever know all the details of what happened back there.'

'If you don't tell anyone what I done with my pa's gang won't you be lying?' Nathaniel asked. 'I thought lawmen always remembered their duty, and never avoided the truth.'

Cassidy laughed, and feeling the

open countryside beginning to warm him, slapped his horse with his hat. As his horse broke into a gallop, he shouted:

'Sounds like you've already learned the first lesson of being a lawman.'

'What's the second lesson?'

Cassidy paused for a moment before answering, and when he did, he spoke to himself as much as he spoke to Nathaniel.

'There is no second lesson.'

Ahead, the trail back to Beaver Ridge beckoned and a return to the normality Cassidy wished he'd never left.

THE END

Other titles in the
Linford Western Library:

STONE MOUNTAIN

Concho Bradley

The stage robbery had been accomplished by an old woman. Twine Fourch had never heard of a female being a highway robber before. He followed the trail all the way to a dilapidated log cabin up Stone Mountain. What happened after that no one could believe even after townsmen from Jefferson found the old log house and the skeletal dying old woman. But before the mystery could be solved there would be two unnecessary killings, a bizarre suicide and a lynching.

GUNS OF THE GAMBLER

M. Duggan

Destitute gambler Ben Crow arrives in Mallory keen to claim his inheritance, only to discover that rancher Edward Bacon has other ideas. Set up by Miss Dorothy, who had fooled him completely, Ben finds himself dangling on the end of a rope. Saved from death, Ben sets off in pursuit of Miss Dorothy, determined upon retribution. However, his quest for vengeance turns into a rescue mission when she is kidnapped by a crazy man-burning bandit.

SIDEWINDER

John Dyson

All Flynn wants is to be Marshal of Tucson, but he is framed by the territory's richest rancher, Frank Buchanan, and thrown into Yuma prison. Five years later Flynn comes out, intent on clearing his name and burning for vengeance. Fists thud, knives flash and bullets fly as he rides both sides of the law and participates in kidnapping and double-dealing. He is once again arrested for a murder of which he is innocent. Can he escape the noose a second time?

THE BLOODING OF JETHRO

Frank Fields

When Jethro Smith's family is murdered by outlaws, vengeance is the one thing on his mind. He meets the brother of one of the murderers, who attempts to exploit Jethro's grudge in the pursuit of his own vendetta. The local preacher, formerly a sheriff, teaches Jethro how to use a gun. With his new-found skills, Jethro and his somewhat unwelcome friend pit themselves against seemingly impossible odds. Whatever the outcome lead would surely fly.

SEVEN HELLS AND A SIXGUN

Jack Greer

Jim Cayman had been warned about Daphne Rankin, his boss's wife, and her little ways. When Daphne made a play for Jim and he resisted, the result was painful and about what he had feared. But suddenly matters went beyond the expected and he found himself left to die an awful death. Only then did he realise that there was far more than a woman scorned. He vowed that if he could escape from the hell-hole he would surely solve the mystery — and settle some scores.

CRISIS IN CASTELLO COUNTY

D. A. Horncastle

The first thing Texas Ranger Sergeant Brad Saunders finds when he responds to an urgent call for help from the local sheriff is the corpse of the public prosecutor floating in the Nueces River. Soon Brad finds himself caught in the midst of a power struggle between a gang of tough western outlaws and a bunch of Italian gangsters, whose thirst for bloody revenge knows no bounds. Brad was going to have all his work cut out to end the bloody warfare — and stay alive!